DeKok and the Dying Stroller

by
BAANTJER

translated from the Dutch by H.G. Smittenaar

INTERCONTINENTAL PUBLISHING

R
fic

BARKING

ISBN 1 881164 09 8

Printing History:
    1st Dutch printing: 1977
    2nd Dutch printing: 1978
    3rd Dutch printing: 1979
    4th Dutch printing: 980
    5th Dutch printing: 1983
    6th Dutch printing: 1984
    7th Dutch printing: 1987
    8th Dutch printing: 1986
    9th Dutch printing: 1988
    10th Dutch printing: 1990
    11th Dutch printing: 1991
    12th Dutch printing: 1992
    13th Dutch printing: 1993

    1st American edition: 1994

Typography: Monica S. Rozier
Cover Photo: Peter Coene

DeKok
and the
Dying Stroller

1

Alex Delzen felt sick. His tanned, athletic body was racked by cold shivers and clammy sweat dripped from his high forehead. His breathing was labored, suffocating . . . and his heart pumped blood through his arteries at an astonishing rate. As far as he could remember, he had only been this sick once before and that was in his childhood when he had eaten some poisoned berries.

He had been barely seven years old and frightened out of his wits when he screamed for his mother. He licked his tongue along dry lips. He would have liked to do it again . . . scream for his mother. But he knew it was useless. His mother was far away. He pressed the palms of his hands tightly against his temples and tried to re-call the vision. But her dear face did not appear. It remained hidden behind a nebulous veil that seemed to restrict his thought processes. He tried again, almost in a panic, with a face that was distorted with pain, but again he failed. Everything remained vague, without contour, without substance. Fear crept up his legs, encircled his chest like a vise and he voiced a single sob. His head seemed to resemble a large, empty globe, filled with the echoes of his throbbing heart. It was as if he had ceased to be a person, had become an empty, hollow, anonymous man . . . without memories.

He wiped the sleeve of his stylish jacket along his forehead and stumbled. His equilibrium seemed disturbed. Staggering, he managed to stay upright.

Suddenly he saw people standing around him, looking at him. Some looked at him with disgust, others seemed amused. Of course, they thought he was drunk, drunk out of his mind. He understood that.

He looked around and decided to explain his situation . . . to tell all these grinning masks, tell them he was not drunk . . . but sick. Sick to death. With one hand he grabbed hold of a passer-by. He opened his mouth and gestured vaguely with his free hand. But there was no sound. His tongue seemed paralyzed and his jaws refused to function. The man he used as support, pushed him roughly away, with a face as if he had just chased away a mangy dog. It hurt. It hurt him terribly. Everything hurt him. He was in agony.

He stopped again after just a few paces. It seemed as if a strangling hand had just squeezed his stomach like a sponge.

The two glasses of cognac that he drank, quickly, one after the other without tasting them, had not helped him at all. He had hoped to give his body some warmth, to get that inner glow he usually achieved after drinking cognac. But that had not happened. On the contrary, cold, icy shivers remained and the cramps increased in severity. He shook his head and wondered what could have happened . . . so suddenly. Only this afternoon he had still felt fine, full of expectations for what the night would bring . . . happy pleasures at the side of a new conquest. He had set out, leisurely strolling toward his appointment, before the delights of the night. Again he tried to find out how it could be possible . . . what had happened. But again he failed. He could no longer control his thoughts, was unable to concentrate. His thoughts wandered, away, far away into a misty world where nothing was recognizable. He closed his eyes, hoping to improve the situation, but a wildly gyrating kaleidoscope was implanted on his retina, reddish, multi-colored, red ... blood red. It was suffocating, frightening. The symmetry of the picture would come and go and then disappear, resolve into a hellish fire ... that chilled.

He walked on like an automaton.

He was on his way to an appointment and he had to keep it, no matter what the cost. He wanted to be on time. It seemed extremely important to him that he should be on time. He looked up. The street was still long, endless ... the Dam, the huge square in front of the Central Railroad Station, was still far, far away.

He was tired, bone-tired. His legs were leaden and only with the greatest difficulty did he manage to drag himself forward. Every step he took was an effort. He gripped his stomach with both hands ... those damn cramps ... the endlessly recurring cramps. He lifted his left arm and looked at his watch ... almost a quarter to eight. He had more than fifteen minutes, but he had to rest, just for a moment. He could afford it. If he could only rest for a few minutes ... just enough to recover, slightly.

He shuffled past some pedestrians and reached the facade of the long street, faltering, stumbling, almost falling. With both hands leaning against a store-window, he rested. The display window was brightly lit and it hurt his eyes. Exactly in front of him he saw a colorful poster ... a slender Eiffel Tower, reaching for the skies. A fat, black strip of lettering underneath. *Eight days Paris*, he read, *four-hundred and fifty guilders*.

He pressed his burning head against the cold glass. A Travel Agency, he realized, I'm standing in front of a Travel Agency. Strange? Happenstance? He grinned. It was a sad grin, full of cynical self-mockery. He was on a voyage, he was traveling, he was departing ... departing for eternity.

9

Slowly he felt consciousness recede and make way for an intense lethargy. Death was mild, he thought, mild and merciful. He was on a journey . . . A Travel Agency nearby.

With half-closed eyes he stared at the display in the window. To the left, a perfect eye-catcher, he discovered a cardboard poster. It depicted a wide, sunny gate with a lot of heavenly blue above. But he could not have come *that* far . . . not already? He was still alive. He could still feel his heartbeat in the tips of his fingers.

Vaguely he read the letters above this new poster. *Come to beautiful Dubrovnik.* The word stabbed his memory. *Dubrovnik* . . . Dubrovnik . . . it sounded so . . . so Russian . . . so melodious . . . so . . .

Suddenly something snapped. The tight, iron band that had imprisoned his thought processes suddenly let go. Slowly the machinery of his brain started to crank up to capacity, with difficulty at first, but very soon it went faster, smoother, he could hear the gears turn. And suddenly, in a blinding flash of insight, he knew truth!

Strong hands gripped him from behind. He looked up. In the reflection of the window he discovered two faces next to his, two faces . . . expressionless, somber faces, faces on top of uniforms. The metal edges of their caps shimmered in the reflection of the Eiffel Tower.

Abruptly everything was clear. The foggy veil around his thoughts evaporated in a clear, fresh breeze that came from nowhere. Suddenly he knew who was responsible for his journey into eternity . . . who was responsible for the poison that slowly flowed through his arteries, spread through his system, slowly, implacably, unstoppable, unrelenting. *He knew who had killed him in cold blood!*

The discovery pained him. It was not so much the thought of death . . . that thought was still too unreal, too insubstantial . . .

but it was the sudden realization of the "why" that saddened him, submerged him into a wave of melancholy. He had to cry. Just cry. His large, brown eyes filled with tears and everything around him started to sparkle, glistened with an unearthly light, thousand upon thousands of stars in a shop window,

They had to know, he thought suddenly. Everybody! He must tell someone, anyone . . . the cops, the people in the street, the people he saw reflected in the window. They had to know who had murdered him and why.

"Raskol," he whispered, softly. "Raskol . . ." he repeated. But that was as far as he went. His mouth refused to obey his will, was unable to form the sounds he needed to produce. His jaws, his tongue . . . they refused. Desperate, with a final, total exertion of his remaining strength, he tried again.

"Raskol . . . Ras . . ." Then he sank into oblivion. His cramped fingers slid down the smooth glass in a last attempt to gain a grip on life, on something, anything . . . then everything became black . . . black as night eternal.

* * *

The two cops in the patrol car were relaxed and at ease as they observed the pedestrians in the long street leading toward the Dam. Then they looked at each other. Diagonally across from them, on the other side of the street, as a disturbing rock in the calm sea of parading pedestrians, they noticed a young man. He swerved from one side of the wide sidewalk to the other and back again. His gait was unsure, almost stumbling. They observed the expensive shoes, the neat pearly-gray suit that had not come off a rack. They also observed how he dragged himself forward, sometimes gesticulating violently in an effort to keep his balance.

Constable First Class Brink turned toward his partner.

"Drunk," he grinned bitterly. "Damn, some people never know their limit . . . I don't mind a few drinks myself . . . but I drink at home, close to my bed." He shook his head. "Just look at him, he needs the entire sidewalk."

His partner at the wheel nodded in agreement. From a professional point of view he was completely of a mind with Constable First Class Brink.

"Let him go for a while," he said, bored with the insignificance of the offence. "Maybe he'll make it. What's the use of a lot of drunks in the cells. They stink up the place and we have to clean up the vomit. It's too early for drunks."

Brink nodded, one eye on the young man on the sidewalk.

"He *is* early," he said, "must have been drinking all afternoon." He looked at his watch "Not even eight yet, barely quarter to."

Constable Vries extracted the small patrol car handily from the stream of traffic and parked at the edge of the sidewalk. From that vantage point they critically observed the behavior of the young man. Their inclination was to pass by, leave well enough alone, but their duty, the responsibility they felt for anything that happened in the streets, prevented them from ignoring the incident.

Brink bit his lips and shook his head.

"He's not going to make it," he observed clinically. "He's too far gone. You watch . . . before you know it he'll be flat on his face. He's as drunk as a sailor after six months at sea."

Vries still tried to soothe the situation.

"Let's wait a little longer," he growled, irritated. "Maybe he'll go into a bar somewhere. At least he'll be off the streets . . . not our worry anymore. Then they can call him a cab and . . ." He did not complete the sentence "How would you like to be a cabdriver?"

Brink did not react. He lost the thread of his partner's words. He opened the door of the car and placed a resolute leg on the pavement.

"We better get him," he worried. "Just to prevent accidents. He's much too close to that display window. Before you know it, he's crashed through it. Shards of glass," he prophesied, " . . . arteries, bleedings . . ."

Brink was possessed of a pessimistic soul and nothing in the streets had ever changed his mind. Fat Vries sighed. Laboriously he struggled from behind the wheel.

"All right, already," he sulked, "but you better keep the desk-sergeant off our backs. He'll be upset, I shouldn't wonder"

* * *

The desk-sergeant was not upset. Calmly he looked up from the Register and observed Brink and Vries as they entered his domain, supporting the drunk between them. He glanced at the young man, turned and grabbed the arrest records from a shelf and slapped it on the desk in front of him, Magically the book opened at the next blank page.

"Drunk?"

Both constables nodded in unison.

"As a skunk."

"Where did you pick him up?"

Brink lifted his cap, wiped the sweat from the inner lining.

"Damrak, near the Dam," he reported. "In front of that Travel Agency. It was *for the safety of self and others,** you see. We were afraid he'd go through the window. He was already leaning against the glass."

The sergeant nodded. Placed a line under his previous notations, looked at the clock and marked the time the drunk had

---
* Actual wording in the instructions for "Constables on Patrol".

13

been brought to his desk. Brink and Vries kept the young man pressed up against the desk to prevent him from falling. The sergeant placed a plastic bag on the desk and motioned for the constables to search the arrestee.

Brink searched the man and emptied his pockets. A wallet, some change, a handkerchief, two unused tickets for the theater . . . everything disappeared in the plastic bag.

The sergeant came from behind the desk, lifted the young man's head by the hair and sniffed.

"He does smell of booze," he said. "What a stink. He must have downed a bottle to be this drunk." He turned the drunk's face toward him. "Hey," he said in a loud tone of voice, "who are you? What's your name?"

The young man groaned and burped, the smell was overpowering. The sergeant turned his head aside and grimaced.

"Take him to a cell," he ordered, "I can't stand the smell."

Brink and Vries took the young man between them and dragged him down the stairs to the cell-block. It was not an easy task, but they were both experienced in handling drunks. They were daily guests at Warmoes Street Station, the busiest police station in Europe. Carefully they manoeuvered the inert figure down the stairs and placed him on a wooden cot in one of the cells. Brink placed a blanket over the body.

Suddenly he leaned closer. The face of the young man bothered him. It was too gray. He unbuttoned the top buttons of the shirt and noticed some tears in the corners of the eyes.

"He's been crying," he said, surprised, but not unduly worried. Drunks often cried. Vries seemed to think so, anyway.

"Crocodile tears," he grinned.

Brink did not laugh. Slowly he rose from his leaning position and he looked down at the supine body with a thoughtful look in his eyes.

"He's been crying," he repeated absent-mindedly.

"So what?"

"Nothing . . . I just hadn't noticed it before. He looks sort of funny, don't you think. Almost unconscious."

"Yes, with booze. He's feeling no pain."

Brink nodded and followed his partner. He hesitated momentarily before closing the cell door.

* * *

Alex Delzen regained consciousness just one more time. For just a moment. Hesitatingly his hand explored the darkness around him. With an effort he opened his eyelids, but it made no difference. The darkness was the same . . . impenetrable. Except for some red dots he did not recognize. He wanted to call out, but the sound stuck in his throat and he remained mute. He did not know what to say, regardless, he thought briefly. He wondered what he would have said if he had been able to do so . . . would he have called somebody . . . who? . . . perhaps his mother.

Suddenly she was there . . . clearly visible and beautiful, as always, in a bright, multi-colored dress. She was right next to him . . . the dearest face in all the world looked at him, surrounded by a heavenly light. She stretched out a hand toward him and motioned. Slowly he rose from the cot and followed the beckoning hand. He recognized the gate, he had seen it before, in a display window. The bright blue sky was there, but behind the gate . . . for the first time he noticed green meadows, inviting, cool, calm green meadows. With a smile on his lips he followed her.

2

Constable Bevers had heard a heavy snoring from cell seven when he made his rounds after the young man had been locked in. Shortly after the change of the watch, the constable noticed that all was silent behind the steel door. He flipped on the light in the cell and peered through the peep-hole. But the sparse lighting in the cell did not reveal anything unusual. Therefore he opened the door to allow the light from the corridor to penetrate the gloom of the cell. The occupant was on his back, partially covered by a blanket. The long, raven hair fell back on either side of his face and there was a strange, almost enraptured smile around his lips. Bevers hesitated. There was something wrong with the situation. He leaned closer and noticed the absence of breathing and the unmistakable pallor of death. He swallowed ... he had been right ... the smile was cold, frozen in place. Carefully the constable went back into the corridor and as was his habit, locked the door with locks, bolts and a drop-bar. Death, too, was not allowed to escape. Pale and upset he reported his finding to the Watch Commander.

The desk-sergeant, accompanied by an older, more experienced constable followed young Bevers to the cells of the ancient police station. The station was so old that the desk-sergeant often compared the cells to dungeons from a less enlightened time. They certainly had not changed for at least a hundred years. Their footsteps echoed against the old, brick walls and the smell of disinfectant permeated everything.

They remained silent and stopped in front of cell seven. Bevers unlocked the door and then swung it open, creaking on its hinges. In turn they took a closer look. The arrestee was dead . . . they all agreed on that. Dead . . . no question about it. It was almost one o'clock in the morning when the Coroner confirmed the opinion and nothing could change that.

* * *

Detective-Inspector DeKok of the Amsterdam Municipal Police (Homicide) waddled into the large detective room of the old, renowned police station at Warmoes Street. His old, decrepit, felt hat was pushed back on his head and he still had his coat on. His upper body was really too large and his legs were proportionally too short. After his fortieth birthday everything seemed to have drooped down to his hips and it gave him a compact, massive, but somewhat comical appearance and slow movements.

The old gray sleuth was in a foul mood. His craggy face with the wrinkles and expression of a good-natured boxer was devoid of his usual friendly good humor. It looked like a thundercloud, grim, full of pent-up energy. An urgent call from the Commissaris, his superior, had woken him from sweet slumber. He had been in the middle of a pleasing dream, in a peaceful world without crime. DeKok had stepped into the real world with the wrong foot, at the wrong side of the bed. He pointed an accusing finger at the clock as he approached his desk, next to that of Vledder, his assistant, colleague and friend.

"Two o'clock," he growled, "two - of - the - clock . . . in the middle of the night, when every good Christian should be in bed

18

and asleep." He snorted. "Whatever does the old man want from us? What could have happened in the middle of the night? Are there no other cops? Besides, I was supposed to have a few days off."

He looked around the busy detective room with obvious disgust. Vledder could almost read his mind. What were all these cops doing here? Could "they" not have picked one from those present?

"The man is dead," sighed Vledder.

DeKok rubbed the bridge of his nose with a little finger.

"Yes, yes," he said, unwilling to be either placated, or interested. "I heard. A man died in the cells downstairs. He isn't the first one and he won't be the last one. It's terribly sad . . . for the deceased . . . but what can I do about it? Is that why they called me? I wasn't there when he got drunk . . . if he hadn't been drunk, they wouldn't have picked him up . . . wouldn't have locked him in and . . . he wouldn't have died. At least, he wouldn't have died in the cell . . . but at home, nice, between clean white sheets, the way you're supposed to die with relatives and loved ones at the foot-end of the bed, discreetly pinking away at hidden tears and wondering about the size of the inheritance."

DeKok went on this way for some time. Vledder waited patiently and with a great deal of apprehension. He had never heard his old mentor carry on this way. It was almost heartless. When DeKok finally wound down, Vledder walked over to the coffeepot and poured a mug of coffee, added a large amount of sugar and placed it in front of the older man.

"Here," said Vledder heartily. "Get yourself around this and don't say anything for a few minutes and then we can talk. Maybe the coffee will cheer you up. I would like to have a *reasonable* conversation."

DeKok gesticulated wildly about.

"*Reasonable*," he exclaimed, "Reasonable! You can't rob an old man like me of his most beautiful dreams and then expect him to be reasonable." He shook his head vehemently. "No, my boy, that's too much to ask. The Commissaris should have realized that. For nightly excursions into criminality you don't want old war-horses like myself. For that you need young, eager beavers such as you."

Vledder sighed again.

"I was Duty Officer," he explained. "Since you were off, they used me for fill-in. That's how I got involved. After they discovered the man they naturally informed me as a matter of course."

"And?"

"Well, I went to look, I looked carefully because the case seemed serious to me, I mean, a man dying in the cells. Then I called the Commissaris at home and asked him to call you."

DeKok sat up abruptly, the mug of coffee forgotten in one enormous hand.

"What!?"

Vledder nodded sheepishly.

"I'm sorry," he said, "But I'm to blame for you being called."

DeKok seemed speechless. He stared at his young colleague with a look of utter astonishment on his craggy face.

"You mean . . . that you . . . you . . ." He did not complete the sentence.

Vledder nervously licked his lips.

"Yes, well, you see . . ." he said hesitatingly, "the fact of the matter is, that it isn't a normal death . . . I think. I mean, it wasn't a natural death . . . to tell you the truth . . . I think . . . I think he's been killed, murdered."

DeKok pushed his lower lip forward, a pugnacious look on his face, a challenge in his eyes.

"I see," he said sarcastically. "And what, may I ask, led you to this conclusion, what stroke of genius convinced you?"

Vledder swallowed.

"Look," he said, "there are circumstances." He sounded unsure of himself. "Nothing that points directly at murder, you understand, nothing concrete. But it's strange. A young man of thirty-two doesn't die, just like that, after a few drinks. I don't believe it. I have a feeling about this . . ." His voice trailed off. He suddenly remembered the many times he had scoffed at "feelings," "intuition" and "instinct".

Something like that must have gone through DeKok's mind.

"Your so-called feelings, cost me a good night's sleep," he jeered.

Young Vledder suddenly pushed his chin further into the room.

"Listen, DeKok," he said sharply. "I didn't ask you to come for nothing. You better believe that. Surely you don't think that I *want* to make a fool out of myself in front of the Commissaris, or you? I'm not crazy! But I say it again . . . that there's something unnatural about the death in that cell. I'm convinced that a crime has been committed. How, or when, or what . . . I don't know. But it's a very strong feeling. Maybe I'm wrong . . . maybe. In that case there's little harm done. But I want to investigate this further. Everybody seems to accept that it just happened. Nobody is thinking of murder and if they are, they're not telling. They were prepared to sweep it under the rug. I had you called because I didn't want it assigned to anybody else, just because you were off. I *want* this case." He pressed his lips together, a stubborn look on his face. DeKok merely stared at him. "And that's the way it is," added Vledder, wanting to add something. "And if you're too grumpy to help me," he concluded, "fine! . . . Then I'll do it by myself."

DeKok continued to stare at him, but his face was no longer expressionless, he looked interested. He had heard a tone of voice from his young friend he had seldom heard before and it surprised him. There was an undertone of annoyance, mixed with quiet determination. It was practically the first time that he had seen Vledder show so much independence and DeKok was very pleased with it. He was so pleased with Vledder's determination that he started to lose his foul mood.

The inner change became clearly visible on his face. The deep creases around his mouth flowed into a fine network of tiny wrinkles and the shadow of a happy and cooperative smile touched his lips. He gestured jovially toward the coffeepot.

"How about another mug of coffee?"

"Coming up," answered Vledder with a sigh of relief.

* * *

DeKok pushed the empty coffee mug aside and placed both legs comfortably on top of his desk. He was again reconciled with life in general and all thoughts of an interrupted night had been pushed into the background. At ease, leaning back in his chair, he watched Vledder who gestured animatedly.

"Please understand, DeKok, I don't want to cause trouble, don't want to seem a smart-aleck, but I've *seen* the corpse in the cell. He was a good-looking guy, well-built, strong, athletic. A man in the bloom of his life." He spread both arms wide. "Of course, that's no guarantee for a long and healthy life ... I understand that, but yet . . . you see, it seems so . . . so unlikely." He paused. "And you're the one who taught me to look for discrepancies, deviations from established patterns," he added cunningly.

"Any outward signs of violence?" asked DeKok, ignoring the implied flattery.

22

"No, but I only looked superficially. We opened his shirt, the desk-sergeant and I. We saw no wounds of any kind, front or back. But then . . . you know how dark the holding cells are."

"Smell anything?"

"Smell of booze, that's all. I mean, nothing specifically, no smell of almonds, or anything like that."

"What did the Coroner say?"

Vledder made a helpless gesture.

"The doctor only looked at the corpse and pronounced it dead. The sergeant asked for a cause of death, but was told to wait for the autopsy."

DeKok nodded thoughtfully.

"Understandable. And, as you say, there were no obvious outward signs of violence . . . we'll just have to wait for the autopsy and the toxicological report. If there has really been a crime, there's only one answer . . . poison."

"That's what I thought," answered Vledder. "It's about the only logical conclusion." He rubbed his chin. "Alcohol is a poison. And the outward signs of alcohol poisoning are called intoxication." He looked at DeKok. "Would there be a big difference."

"How do you mean?"

"Well, between alcohol poisoning and poisoning by some other means."

"That depends on the nature of the poison, the quantity, possibly the combination of more than one poison. But to a certain extent the symptoms are similar, at least with relatively slow-working poisons."

Vledder nodded, as if DeKok had confirmed his own thoughts.

"So, in retrospect it isn't all that strange that he was picked up for being drunk in public. He must have displayed all the classic symptoms of a drunk. The desk recorded him as having been arrested *for the safety of self and others*, but the sergeant listed him as drunk. Stumbling gait . . . raving . . . whatever."

DeKok looked up.

"Raving? Did he say anything?"

"No, I'm assuming that. According to the sergeant, he didn't say a word."

"What about the crew that brought him in?"

"Brink and Vries. They had long since gone home by the time I was notified. Their tour was over at eleven. I'll talk to them tomorrow. I was thinking of getting a more detailed report from them, anyway. I mean, it's no longer a case of just one more drunk, after all."

"Yes," agreed DeKok. "They probably have to justify the arrest in more detail. You watch. The Desk-sergeant, Bikerk was it? Yes. He'll have to come up with a few more details as well. He ordered the lock-up. This is inevitably going to be leaked to the papers and then come the inevitable headlines. I can see them now: *Man Dies In Cell, Inadequate Surveillance? Was Medical Assistance Denied?* Oh yes, the papers will have a field-day with it. I've seen it before. And you can bet your bottom dollar that the Commissaris will want to know every little detail. The old man is scared stiff of the press."

Vledder flared up.

"But surely it's nobody's fault. Certainly they can't blame the police!"

DeKok raised a restraining hand.

"Hush, I didn't say that. In fact, I'm not at all concerned about who's at fault. It's the fault of the system. But what do you want, cops aren't doctors. It shouldn't have happened. If, as you suspect, a man has been poisoned and as a result thereof is found stumbling around the streets, it's a sad state of affairs that the police, who are there to protect the public, lock him up as a drunk, leaving him to die, alone, lonely and forgotten."

Vledder listened with amazement. This new diatribe was in direct contrast with the earlier, cynical remarks. The difference was, realized Vledder, that at that time DeKok had *sounded* angry but probably was not. This time he sounded resigned, but Vledder noticed a seething cauldron of anger and frustration beneath the calm sounds of the words. He had learned to be sensitive to his mentor's moods and feelings.

"Yes," agreed Vledder, "you're right. It's sad, terribly sad. You should be able to forget about it, but it's enough to make you want to accuse the whole system." He stared in the distance. Then he continued, thoughtfully: "You wonder how you can prevent it from happening again."

DeKok shrugged his shoulders in apparent unconcern. He was unable to fool Vledder this time.

"Ach," DeKok said quietly, "Those things happen . . . with the best of intentions . . . at least, we must hope so."

"To serve the public," grinned Vledder cynically.

3

DeKok ambled over to the coffee pot and poured himself another mug of coffee.

"What do we know about the victim?" he asked.

"Not much," answered Vledder, scratching the back of his neck in a subconscious imitation of one of DeKok's habits. "I took a good look at his clothes and stuff. Everything is of first quality, perhaps just a little obvious, a couple of hundred in the wallet, a number of Gold Cards and identity papers in the name of Alex Delzen."

DeKok's eyebrows rippled suddenly. It was a startling sight. Nobody had ever been able to describe the movements exactly, but DeKok's eyebrows seemed to lead a life of their own. This time they most resembled two hairy caterpillars marching in place. Every time again, Vledder was both startled and fascinated by the phenomenon.

"Alex Delzen," repeated DeKok pensively. "I've heard that name before . . . or read it somewhere. I just can't place it right now. How old is he?"

"Thirty-two."

"What does he do for a living?"

"Student."

"A bit old for a student, don't you think?" laughed DeKok.

"Well, he has a current Student I.D. from the Free University, so it's probably right. Also, he lives, or lived, at the Brewers Canal. You know, the small, narrow house, almost at the corner of the Prince's Canal. As far as I know it's a student place, I mean, a lot of students live there in rooms." He chewed the end of a pencil. "What do you call a bunch of students like that?"

"A gaggle?" joked DeKok.

"No, no, let me think. A fraternity . . . a study group . . . come on, it's on the tip of my tongue."

"A cluster," supplied DeKok, "in Holland we call that a cluster, indicating a small sub-group of a larger organization."

"No, that wasn't it. It had another name, let me check my notes."

"Dispute?" asked DeKok, while Vledder flipped pages.

"That's it, I have it here some place."

"Dispute," mused DeKok, " . . . well, I suppose so, it's rather old-fashioned, you know. There was a time when students gathered to practice their 'disputes' on each other, from 'disputation', meaning an academic exercise involving the arguing of a thesis between its maintainer and opponents. But I don't think it's been called a *dispute* for years. Too confusing, you see. I like *cluster* better."

"Yes, yes," agreed Vledder absent-mindedly, taking DeKok's knowledge of trivia in stride, "but *they* called it a Dispute, at least officially. There were some letters to that effect, a debating society of sorts, a dispute. Right, here it is, it had a name too. *Disputa Hora Ruit*."

DeKok looked interested.

"A good name," he said admiringly. "You know what it means?"

"No . . . I was never that good in Latin."

"*Time passes*."

28

"How appropriate."

"I like it," said DeKok, raking his fingers through his hair. "Yessir, I like it. *Hora Ruit*." He savored the words. "Very nice." Then he gestured in Vledder's direction. "Anything else?"

"A couple of pamphlets exhorting student protests of one kind or another and two unused tickets for the theater."

"What theater, what performance?"

Vledder consulted his notebook.

"September thirteen, Amsterdam Theater for the Performing Arts. William Shakespeare's *Much Ado About Nothing*. It's tonight."

"You mean last night . . ."

"Yes, of course, last night. Curtain was at eight thirty, but the tickets were bought several days ago."

"How do you know?"

"Well, we weren't, aren't officially assigned to the case yet, so I took what notes I could. All the evidence is still downstairs, of course. The tickets seemed significant, so I wrote down the numbers and checked them out."

"At this hour?"

"Oh, yes, the performance wasn't over until after midnight and there were still people in the office when I called."

"Hm. Well, it looks as if Alex Delzen was on his way to a date, an appointment surely, and had planned a visit to the theater." He looked up. "He was brought in at eight, right?"

Again Vledder consulted his notebook.

"Yes, the notes in the drunk register read as follows: *Twenty hours, cell seven, man locked in under article 453 to sober up. Too drunk to give his name.*"

DeKok sighed deeply.

"Poor fellow," he said, pity in his voice, "he never made it."

Vledder shook his head, agreeing with the sentiment.

"It would be nice to know who was waiting for him, who he was meeting."

"In other words, for whom was the second ticket?"

"Yes, he, or she, waited in vain."

DeKok rose slowly from his chair and walked over to the window. There he stood, looking out into the street, slowly bouncing up and down on the balls of his feet. Downstairs, he saw a cream-colored ambulance, the rear-doors open. The victim was being removed. Two constables helped with the transfer. DeKok stared pensively at the rooftops across the street, completely oblivious to the constant hubbub in the noisy room behind him.

"*Hora Ruit,*" he murmured. "But not for Alex Delzen. For him the bell tolled . . . *Hora Est.*"

"*Hora Est?*" questioned Vledder.

"It is time," nodded DeKok.

* * *

Commissaris* Buitendam, the tall, stately Chief of Warmoes Street Station did not look like the Chief of the busiest police station in Europe. He looked like a distinguished diplomat of the old school, always elegant and immaculately dressed, with gray-flecked hair and the long, slender hands of a pianist. By nature, too, he was more a diplomat, a politician, than he was a policeman. At least, reflected DeKok ruefully, ever since he had reached his exalted rank.

DeKok remembered his Chief as a competent cop, albeit overly concerned with rules and regulations, an almost

---

* Commissaris: a rank equivalent to Captain. There are only two ranks higher: Chief-Commissaris and Chief Constable. Each jurisdiction has only a single Chief Constable, the highest possible police rank. There is one Chief Constable for all of Amsterdam. Other ranks in the Municipal Police are: Constable, Constable First Class, Sergeant, Adjutant, Inspector, Chief-Inspector and Commissaris. Adjutants and below are equivalent to non-commissioned ranks. Inspector is a rank equivalent to 2nd Lieutenant.

pathological insistence on reports and an urgent desire to be kept informed on the smallest details. At times there was a lot of the early Commissaris in young Vledder, thought DeKok. He faced his Chief with quiet resignation. He owed it to the man's position, but DeKok, protected in a cocoon of seniority and a long string of brilliant successes, was not overly concerned.

Although he would never rise above his present rank, a fact to which DeKok was supremely indifferent, he also knew the Commissaris could not fire him. Could not even transfer him without looking foolish. The average tenure of an officer at the busy Warmoes Street station was five years. DeKok had been there for more than thirty years, almost twenty-five years in Homicide. DeKok was a jewel in the commissarial crown and deep down both men knew it.

The Commissaris excitedly waved a morning paper about.

"This," he said in his affected, la-di-da voice, "is the limit. The ab - so - lute limit." He waved the paper for emphasis. "I have never, in my entire career, encountered the like. It's one thing that the public, the papers criticize us . . . it's a fact of life and we'll have to live with it. After all, we *do* live in a democracy." He slapped the paper on the edge of his desk. "But this . . . this . . ."

DeKok was confused.

"What?" he managed to ask.

The Chief threw the newspaper at his subordinate.

"Read the front page! It is clearly suggested that *we*, the police, have murdered Alex Delzen!"

"Us!?"

The Commissaris nodded vehemently.

"Murdered! We just tossed him in a cell and let him die! On purpose. Not of our own accord, oh no, but on orders! On quiet and secret instructions from a reactionary government that feared the growing influence of Delzen's genius!"

"What rot."

"Indeed, I couldn't agree with you more. But the public reads this . . . this . . ."

"Delzen is supposed to be a genius?" asked DeKok incredulously. "I thought he was just a perfect example of the eternal student, that's all. A genius . . . I doubt it."

"He was one of those . . . those," the Commissaris gesticulated. ". . . One of those politically correct activists, the type that has always brought unrest to the student world. He was considered to be one of the prime movers behind a number of student riots."

"That's no reason to kill him," shrugged DeKok.

The Commissaris sank down in his chair.

"No, not for us," he agreed. "And most certainly not for the Government. But apparently there are certain groups who'd like nothing better than to saddle us with having murdered Alex Delzen. It's just grist for their mill. You see, DeKok, Delzen's death may have serious political repercussions."

"We're just cops," growled DeKok. "Just simple cops who try to do their duty. What have we got to do with politicians?" He pronounced the last word as if he had spoken an obscenity. "Let the papers write what they want."

"Whether you like it or not," said his boss, shaking his head, "the politicians are interested in us. Let's hope, for all our sakes, that the unfortunate young man in cell seven died a natural death." He leaned forward, stretched out a hand toward DeKok. "But," he continued, "if it turns out he has been murdered, as young Vledder suggests, it is of primary importance to apprehend the murderer as soon as possible. Rather today than tomorrow. We owe it to ourselves."

"Why?"

"Why? . . . Why?" The Commissaris swallowed, had difficulty speaking. "Why?" he asked again, sharply. "Because I don't want any trouble. I've already been flooded with phone calls from all sorts of important people . . . because I don't intend to be the scapegoat for some political game! You understand?"

DeKok shook his head.

"No," he answered calmly, stubbornly, "no, I don't understand."

The Commissaris closed his eyes and sighed.

"Just go," he said in a tired, resigned tone of voice. "I'll await your reports."

DeKok left the room, a sly smile on his face.

* * *

Vledder looked at his old partner with a look of half-amused exasperation on his face.

"You just can't control yourself, can you? The old man is sitting on a bed of coals, you should have some sympathy for that. Alex Delzen's death is politically explosive."

"So what," snorted DeKok. "As I told the boss, I'm a cop. I investigate crimes. That's my job. That has nothing to do with politics. A surgeon doesn't ask if his patient is politically left, right, or what's the term these days . . . oh, yes . . . correct. He just cuts away." The gray sleuth gestured wildly. "And that's me. If a crime has been committed, I just cut away. If Alex Delzen has been murdered, I will find his killer, regardless of any political interests, implications, or motives, be they left, right or . . . correct."

"You're strange man, DeKok, and that you are," said Vledder.

"Fine," answered the older man, "let's leave it at that." He waved the subject into oblivion. "Let's get to business . . . what about the autopsy?"

Vledder shrugged his shoulders.

"Nothing special. Alex Delzen was whole, on the inside as well as the outside. Dr. Rusteloos could discover no physical reasons for a sudden death. According to Dr. Rusteloos, he died of poisoning."

"But he couldn't prove it?"

"No, tissue samples and such were sent to Dr. Eskes in Forensic. He'll do the toxicological research. He's also looking into stomach content, urine samples, you name it."

"What else?

"Like I said, tissues . . . liver, kidneys, lungs . . ."

"Yes, yes," waved DeKok, "that's not what I meant. What about puncture marks?"

"No, Dr, Rusteloos looked very carefully, as you might expect, but there were no puncture marks, either recent, or from an earlier date. As far as could be determined, he did not do drugs and wasn't poisoned by injection."

* * *

DeKok lifted his ridiculous little hat.

"My dear Dr. Eskes," he said humbly. "Do forgive me for intruding on your preserve, but do you have any news?" He made a helpless gesture. "How far have you progressed with the toxicological findings? You understand that I'm curious. I really would like to know for sure if Delzen has been murdered, or not."

Dr. Eskes, one of the foremost forensic specialists in the Netherlands, placed a friendly arm around DeKok's shoulders and led him toward an untidy office, off to the side of the large, gleaming laboratory space. Behind the office was a smaller, private laboratory where Dr. Eskes did most of his work, leaving the modern, shiny space to his assistants and students. In his heart Dr. Eskes was an alchemist, born five hundred years too late. Perhaps that was why he and DeKok liked each other so much. DeKok, too, was born too late. He longed for the days of stage coaches and when the fastest and most comfortable means of transportation was a barge, pulled by a fast horse, along one of the many canals or rivers of Holland. Like Dr. Eskes, he tolerated and used modern technology, but was never able to really appreciate it.

"Yes, my dear DeKok," answered Dr. Eskes, "I'm fully cognizant of your desire to know more about the circumstances. If my research were to reveal that Alex died a natural death, your further involvement would, perforce, be superfluous. You can set it aside, so to speak." He looked at his old friend with a twinkling in his eyes. "And of course, down deep among your innermost thoughts, you hope that there will be no indications of poisoning. I would not, in the least, be surprised if you were to have little stomach for yet another murder case."

"You know me too well, doctor," grinned DeKok.

The forensic expert smiled.

"Yes, indeed, and I have known you for a long time as well. I remember your first case as if it were yesterday." With a shock DeKok realized that the youthful looking man must be in his eighties. "Believe me, when I say," continued Dr. Eskes, "that I recollect with clarity every single one of the murders you have solved. There were, to say the least, a number of them. And let me also add that I have always had the greatest admiration for the manner in which you brought all of them to a successful conclusion. Yes, you have been *very* successful."

DeKok stared at the jumble in the crowded office.

"Yes," he agreed tiredly. "Successful. Perhaps you won't believe me, but I'm not all that happy about that. You see, being successful creates obligations, expectations. Sometimes I've the feeling I'm always walking on eggshells."

"An uncomfortable form of locomotion."

DeKok ignored the joking remark.

"You know what I mean. Sometimes I have the feeling that people look at me like some sort of freak, some . . . clairvoyant with paranormal gifts. And you, better than most, know that the solving of murders has little to do with crystal balls." He paused, scratched the back of his neck. "Sometimes I wonder what would happen if I failed, if I didn't catch the perpetrator. I don't think anyone can imagine such a thing." He paused again and looked at the old doctor. "Personally, you're right, I do hope sincerely that Delzen was *not* murdered."

"I understand the dilemma," responded the doctor sympathetically. "You would be forced, once again, to demonstrate your undoubted ability. To perform up to expectations." He lowered himself into a chair, casually brushing some papers onto the floor. "But I am sorry, DeKok, truly, I regret it most sincerely. I have to disappoint you. Although the research has not yet been completed . . . I await the result of a few reactions . . . but I can tell you that the stomach and intestines of the deceased contained a fatal amount of diethylparanitrofenulthiophosphate."

DeKok's eyebrows rippled briefly.

"Contained what?"

"Diethylparanitrofenulthiophosphate," laughed Dr. Eskes. "Almost impossible to pronounce, but you will be able to do so, with a little practice. There are only thirty-four letters. Just count them."

"I wouldn't think about it."

The forensic expert laughed again.

"But it's just that way, no need to break your jaw over it. I will write it correctly in my detailed analysis. You should have no trouble copying it for your report."

"And . . . what is this diethyl-stuff?"

Dr. Eskes reached out, seemingly at random, and pulled a pamphlet from a laden shelf.

"Diethylparanitrofenulthiophosphate," he read without hesitation, "is the catalyst ingredient for parathion, a poison used in agriculture, belonging to the group of organic phosphoric-acid esters with anti-cholesteric effects."

"Well, it's all Greek to me," grinned DeKok, "pure abracadabra. But it sounds very good . . . impressive." He looked at the older man, a twinkling in his eyes. "If," he continued, "we delete all the ruffles and flourishes, are we then left with just parathion?"

Dr. Eskes nodded calmly.

"Essentially correct," he answered. "Parathion is an extremely lethal poison, whether taken orally, or by inhalation. It can, in certain cases, permeate the skin with lethal results."

"Frightening. What about the symptoms?"

"Headache, dizziness, nausea, constricted sensation of the chest area, restlessness, frightening hallucinations, tears and impairment of vision," he recited without looking at his notes. "In later stages," he lectured on, "the symptoms will be acerbated by severe cramps of the stomach, diarrhea, heavy perspiration and painful contractions of the abdominal muscles."

"Vile stuff," said DeKok, a distasteful look on his face.

"Yes," agreed Dr. Eskes. "A vile substance indeed. Two hundred and fifty milligrams is already a lethal . . . a deadly dose. And to think that this extremely dangerous poison is readily available to thousands, tens of thousands of people. By the liter. Generally it is stored under the kitchen sink, or in a shed in the garden, readily accessible to anyone. It is a disturbing thought. It's essentially an insecticide, but people use it also as a weedkiller."

They remained silent for several minutes. DeKok searched his pockets for some hard candy of which he seemed to carry around an inexhaustible supply. He found a piece, peeled of the wrapper and placed the sweet in his mouth.

"Parathion," he said thoughtfully. "A bit unusual, surely. I mean . . . for the city. I've never run across it in Amsterdam."

The police expert shook his head.

"No," he agreed, "No. I cannot recall a single instance in an urban area." He smiled faintly. "But, as I said, it is an agrarian poison and the average Amsterdammer is city-born and bred. However," he continued didactically, "In the country a lot of accidents have been known to happen involving this lethal substance. One needs merely to glance at the newspaper articles. It is also often used for murder. It is rather fast acting."

"How fast?"

"That, of course, depends on the dosage. The time may vary from a few minutes to several hours. It depends on several circumstances."

"Such as?"

"First of all," lectured Dr. Eskes, "there is the quantity. Then the resistance of the potential victim and the victim's physical condition. Another, by no means unimportant factor, how much did the victim eat and or drink shortly before the poison was introduced into the system. Some edibles and certain beverages can have a delaying influence. Others may speed up the process . . . alcohol, for instance."

DeKok nodded his understanding.

"Did Delzen have alcohol in the blood? The desk-sergeant and the arresting officers seemed convinced that he smelled of alcohol."

"Yes," said Dr. Eskes, tapping a pile of papers. "There was alcohol in the bloodstream. Somewhere here are my notes . . ." He glanced at the various piles of paper on his desk and then made another, unerring selection. "Here we are," he said. "It was 0.65 *pro mille*, a little more than 0.005 percent."

"Two or three drinks," said DeKok thoughtfully. "Not much."

"You are correct, a minute amount as these things are measured. But sufficient to considerably speed up the effect of the parathion . . . it facilitated absorption into the bloodstream."

"Would it be possible to come up with some sort of time frame?"

"I would be careful about times, were I you," advised the doctor. "For instance, we are not sure about the exact time of death. Yes, I know," he said, raising a restraining hand, "sometime between eight and midnight. But that is about all we know. If you want to work your way back to the time of ingestion of the poison, it behooves you to take a very wide latitude into consideration, or one may be faced with unexpected, unpleasant surprises."

"Poisonings," exclaimed DeKok angrily. "Good thing it happens so seldom."

Dr. Eskes rose from his chair, walked over to the window and looked out over the rooftops of the old city.

"I would be careful about such statements, were I you," he said softly.

"What do you mean, doctor?"

"I believe that we, the police, have no idea about the exact quantity of poisonings that happen on a regular basis."

DeKok gestured impatiently.

"Ach," he said, shrugging his shoulders, "There can't be that many. When is the last time you heard about a poisoning? They're few and far between. Maybe one, or two, per year."

Dr. Eskes turned around and looked at him.

"You are correct . . . according to the statistics. But," he raised a finger into the air. "One should realize that the statistics only reflect the number of poisonings of which we are aware, when the victim has been subjected to an autopsy *and* a

39

toxicological investigation. We know nothing about other cases."

"I don't follow you," admitted DeKok and he was not referring to the good doctor's penchant for using multi-syllable words. "Of course we're not aware of all cases. After all, we only know about the poisonings we discover. The rest will remain a secret. That's the same for all crime. There's always a missing link . . . a hidden fact, or . . . an incompetent policeman."

"Exactly," declared Dr. Eskes. "But that is the thrust of my argument. I consider the number of undiscovered poisonings to be disproportionally high."

"Really?" questioned DeKok. "You can't mean that there are a high number of cases that are never discovered? People who are buried routinely, without further investigation, while in fact they have been calmly killed?"

"Calmly is an understatement. But that is exactly what I mean."

"But, but, that's too . . . too absurd." DeKok was stunned. "Whatever gave you that idea?"

"Not absurd at all, my dear DeKok. No, not absurd whatsoever. It is a considered and justified conclusion. As my point of departure," he explained, "I used the number of attempts."

"Attempts?"

"Yes, the number of *attempted* poisonings happens to be rather high. You would be amazed if you knew how many times a person attempts to poison another. And not only in the Netherlands. It is the same all over the world, wherever such statistics are maintained." The old man sat down, prepared to discuss the problem at length.

"An *attempted* poisoning is a murder that did not succeed," he began. "It is discovered in time. And how is it discovered? In other words . . . what is the origin of the discovery. Well, the

40

potential victim does not feel well and visits a doctor. In some cases the victim will mention the possibility of poisoning, in other cases an alert physician may observe the symptoms. People may speak of 'food-poising', or say they ate something 'that did not agree with them'. Whatever the reason, it is always the victim who sets in motion the chain of events that will, eventually, lead to a criminal investigation." He paused briefly. "But what happens," he asked rhetorically, "if the victim is no longer able to communicate? In other words, if the *attempted* poisoning was *successful*?" Dr. Eskes grinned broadly and answered his own questions. "Then, my dear friend, nobody knows, not even the famous DeKok."

DeKok smiled faintly.

"I think," he said pensively, "that you're oversimplifying things. A poisoning, a successful poisoning isn't all that simple. First you have to get hold of the poison, then you have to trick your victim . . . nobody takes poison voluntarily. And if all that works, you have to avoid the doctor. I mean, when one of his, or her, patients suddenly dies, the average doctor is going to be reluctant to casually issue a Death Certificate. If they are not completely sure, have the tiniest bit of doubt, they'll summon the Coroner and request an autopsy." He sighed deeply. "But you're right . . . if one is careful, a well-prepared poisoning can easily remain undiscovered."

"Blood chills at the thought," commented old Dr. Eskes.

They remained silent until a smile suddenly lit up the doctor's face.

"You know, DeKok, whenever I talk about poison, I am inevitably reminded of that play, *Arsenic and old lace*, wherein two dear old ladies calmly do away with about a dozen lonely, old men . . . because they are so lonely and unhappy. Priceless. And in our own country we had 'Sweet Mina' the caring poison mixer from Leiden who wiped out five families for the insurance

41

money. They called her 'Sweet Mina' because she was always so sweet, caring and friendly. In the neighborhood where she practiced her nefarious activities she was known as an 'Angel of Mercy'." The police expert placed his index finger at the tip of his nose. "You see, DeKok, that is one of the clues. People who poison other people often have a very humane, compassionate and friendly mask behind which they hide."

"A friendly mask," repeated DeKok quietly. "I wonder what kind of mask Delzen's killer used."

"It would simplify matters considerably," commented Dr. Eskes, "if one knew."

4

DeKok stood in his favorite spot, in front of the window of the large detective room, quietly rocking on the balls of his feet while he looked out over the rooftops of the Quarter. He looked at his friend Moshe, the herring man, who manoeuvred his cart out of Corner Alley and thought with regret that it had been a long time since he had tasted a fresh, raw herring. At least a day, or so. His mouth watered at the memory.

The area he was looking at consisted, in DeKok's mind, of the famous, or infamous, depending on one's point of view, Red Light District of Old Amsterdam. The district encompassed a veritable labyrinth of narrow streets, small canals, quaint old bridges, dark alleys, unexpected squares and architectural wonders. All enlivened by thousands of exotic, often beautiful ladies, well-dressed pimps, innumerable bars and eating establishments of every kind. The endless streams of the sexually deprived, or those who thought they were and, of course, the bus loads of tourists from all over the world and the seamen from every nationality mixed with the locals of the centuries old quarter to create an atmosphere which could not be duplicated anywhere else in the world.

He had spent many years in and around the Quarter and he knew almost everybody there, that is to say, almost everybody in the Quarter knew him. He was neither feared, nor notorious. He was simply accepted as just another facet, a different facet because he represented the Law, but another facet all the same, of the exquisite melange that offered so much pleasure, while hiding so much pain and sorrow.

On the whole DeKok was well liked. The pimps and the whores and the other shady denizens of the District treated him with respect. They knew he administered the law in a supple way, that he interpreted the dozens of regulations and guidelines with a certain latitude that was, although not in direct violation of the *spirit* of the law, perhaps to be considered as a unique vision on the *letter* of the law.

DeKok was a concept to them, like Moshe and like Little Lowee, the owner and operator of DeKok's favorite bar.

Slowly he turned around and approached Vledder's desk. As usual the younger man was doing something incomprehensible on his computer. DeKok had never discovered the fascination of the device. His own terminal was carelessly pushed to a corner of his desk. Occasionally he used it as a convenient resting place for his coffee mug.

"Alex Delzen," he began nonchalantly, "was indeed murdered . . . poisoned. Dr. Eskes found traces of parathion."

Vledder looked up from his work. Surprised and delighted.

"So . . . after all."

"Yes."

The young Inspector laughed out loud.

"What did I tell you?" It sounded enthusiastic, almost challenging and just a little smug. "What did I tell you? Not a natural death, but murder . . . poison. I knew it. I just knew it. There was something wrong about the body." Vledder looked at his colleague. "You'll have to admit that I was right."

DeKok pursed his lips and seemed to think before answering.

44

"I admit it," he said calmly. "Of course I admit it. You've been extremely alert and you're making progress. Before you know it you'll be a real detective. Just a few more years."

Vledder seemed deflated. DeKok was amused.

"A few more years," fumed Vledder, accepting DeKok's judgement, but unable to refrain from protesting. "A few more years . . . I thought I knew quite a bit, already. I mean, we've solved a respectable number of cases together . . . the somber nude, the dead harlequin, the sorrowing tomcat, the disillusioned corpse . . . the list is long, recently the case with that nurse and I've been watching you carefully, DeKok. They were all difficult cases and I watched you, learned from you. I really thought I had progressed further. That's why I thought I could tackle this by myself."

"Tackle what?"

"This murder."

"Then why did you have me called in?"

"The excitement of the moment."

"And you called me a strange man."

"Well . . ."

DeKok went to his own desk and lowered himself into the chair. From behind his unused terminal he peered at his young colleague.

"You think you can handle it?"

"Yes," answered Vledder with confidence.

DeKok raked his fingers through his hair, lost in thought. Vledder studied the face of his old mentor with tense expectation. He looked at the network of friendly creases, the somewhat broad nose, the firm chin and he was again struck by the resemblance to a good-natured boxer. But he could not detect an identifiable expression. It made him nervous and irritated.

"Well?" he demanded.

DeKok chewed his lower lip.

"This is going to be a difficult case," he said in a fatherly tone of voice. He sounded convincing. "A case with many aspects, unexpected twists. Believe me, poisonings are always difficult. You shouldn't underestimate the difficulties ..." He looked away and smiled. "They're poison." He paused and looked at Vledder who looked back expectantly. "A poisoner is difficult to catch. He, or she, is a troublesome and above else ... a dangerous opponent. Poisoners are cunning and sly by nature and almost impossible to recognize."

Vledder shrugged his shoulders with youthful confidence.

"What's the difference. Whether the murder weapon is a gun, a scarf, a knife, a hockey stick or ... poison. Murder is murder." He gestured vaguely. "And I have never heard of a murderer who, just to please us, wrote 'guilty' on his forehead." He looked at DeKok, a twinkling in his eyes. "To paraphrase something you once said," he added.

DeKok was serious.

"No," he said, "they're usually not that obliging."

"All right, then," exclaimed Vledder eagerly. "What's the difference ... murder by poison, or murder by some other means. The procedures are the same."

DeKok listened carefully to the sharp tones. He studied Vledder. A single glance was enough. He recognized the look of stubborn, determined resolve. DeKok sighed deeply. He would have to get used to it.

"So, you think you can tackle it on your own? You think you can find Alex Delzen's murderer?"

"Yes," said Vledder tersely.

DeKok rubbed the bridge of his nose with a little finger. It took several seconds, then he lifted the finger in the air and stared at it as if he had never seen it before. He had reached a conclusion.

"Very well," he said, "go ahead."

Vledder had the grace to blush.

"You mean ..."

"Exactly what I'm saying. As of now you're in charge of the investigation. I ... eh, I will assist you." He made a comical gesture. "All right, chief, what's on the menu? What should I do? Who do you want me to arrest?" It sounded forced.

Vledder looked at his old colleague with a certain amount of suspicion. He saw the somber look on his face and drew the wrong conclusion.

"Please don't be angry, DeKok," he apologized. "I don't want that. Really, that wasn't my intention. I like you too much for that, you should know that, but ..." He stopped, searching for the right words. "You have to understand, I don't want a new partner. But I *have* to prove, sooner or later, that I can do it ... even without your help. That's all. This poisoning business seems to be right up my alley. I think I can solve it.'

"I'm not angry," denied DeKok, shaking his head. "Never with you. If you see possibilities in this case, then you must pursue them. As far as that's concerned ..." He made a languid, almost sad gesture. "I'd be the last person to stand in the way of your career."

Vledder swallowed.

"Then you don't mind if I try it by myself for a while? Just to see how far I get? You understand, just for my own satisfaction."

DeKok pushed his lower lip forward and shook his head.

"No," he answered quietly. "You go ahead. I'll clear it with the old man. He can make it official, that'll be best. I still have some days off coming. I think I'll use them."

A relieved smile appeared on Vledder's face.

"You're a great man, DeKok," he said, "and that you are."

"Yes," said DeKok, "I've been told."

He picked his hat off the coat-rack in passing and ambled out of the room.

5

"I don't like it." Commissaris Buitendam shook his head. "No, indeed, I don't like it at all. This case is too serious . . . too delicate. I simply cannot afford to leave it in the hands of a young, inexperienced officer."

"Vledder isn't inexperienced," answered DeKok firmly. "He and I have worked together for years. It's about time we let him operate on his own."

"Not in this case."

DeKok did not seem to hear his boss.

"I'm a bit tired," he said after a long pause. "I don't think I'm altogether fit for duty." He felt his head tenderly. "I'm due for a vacation. I've also piled up a lot of compensation days."

The Commissaris looked at him searchingly.

"Are you telling me that you . . . no matter what . . . that you are *not* prepared to handle the Delzen case?"

DeKok scratched the back of his neck.

"I just want a few days off," he scowled. "Is that so strange?"

"But you almost never take off," protested the Commissaris. "When you do go, you have to be practically forced to do so."

DeKok did not answer. The police chief stared at his subordinate, while he nervously tapped the top of his desk with a long, aristocratic finger. But he knew he was defeated. An unwilling DeKok was worse than no DeKok at all.

"I understand," capitulated the Chief, finally. "Any further discussion will be useless. There's no talking to you." He nodded to himself. "All right then . . . I'll instruct Vledder to take over the case. Perhaps it's better. This political climate is not exactly your cup of tea. Besides . . . students are mostly young people and . . ."

DeKok looked up.

"And I'm an old man?" It sounded cynical and sad.

The Commissaris did not know what to say.

* * *

The charming and ever young Mrs. DeKok looked surprised when her husband came home at two in the afternoon.

"You're early."

DeKok threw his hat at the peg in the corridor and pulled off his coat with tired, slow movements.

"Do you have to go out again, tonight?"

He kissed her on the forehead.

"No, I'm not going out tonight. I'm staying home with you. I'm off."

"Off?"

"Yes, just off." He sounded irked.

A deep crease appeared on her forehead.

"Is . . . eh, is the murder of that student already solved, then? I thought you had just started on that? Yesterday you weren't even sure if it was murder."

DeKok leaned over and stroked the head of his faithful dog, a boxer. There were some who maintained that DeKok looked like his dog and others were convinced that the dog looked like DeKok. Whatever the viewpoint, there was a remarkable similarity between DeKok and his dog.

"Vledder has the case."

She looked at him with uncomprehending eyes.

"Vledder has the case . . . why?"

He avoided looking at her.

"The boy was really keen on it." He sounded as if he was talking about a whining child. "He thinks he can handle it . . . on his own." He paused, looked at her. "So, what could I do? I should be happy. I've trained him in the hope that he would, eventually, replace me. So I could take it easier." He made a vague gesture, stroked his dog again. "Well, the moment has arrived."

"But you don't like it?" she asked tenderly.

DeKok grinned foolishly.

"Perhaps it doesn't sound very nice . . . but, you're right, to be absolutely honest about it . . . No, indeed, I don't like it all." He suddenly realized he had used the same words as his boss, not too long ago. He grinned to himself. "To tell you the truth," he continued, "it gives me a funny feeling inside. It's as if I died . . . just a little. You understand . . . finished, like an old steam locomotive on a forgotten track. Superfluous."

She smiled sweetly.

"And now you've taken some time off to get used to the idea."

DeKok sat down in an easy chair and pushed his always tender feet into a pair of comfortable slippers.

"A few days. It's about time I take another look at my rods. I think I'll go fishing. Bert, Bert Berends discovered a spot in the north of the province that's full of the most beautiful pikes. They're just waiting in line, he said, you practically have to give them numbers, or they'll crowd your hook." He scratched the back of his neck. "Yessir, I think I'm going to take a look there. If I hang around the station I'll get involved, no matter what. I know how that goes. I just couldn't control myself." He looked at her fondly. "That's why I took some time off. He's got to have a fair chance. He's earned it."

She had seated herself across from him, listening intently, her hands in her lap. She knew all about DeKok's professional life, his ups and downs. After more than thirty years of marriage, they had become a part of her as well.

"What did the Commissaris have to say about it?"

DeKok shrugged his shoulders.

"He didn't like the idea, resisted it. He had all sorts of objections."

"And?"

"I told him Vledder could handle it. That he was ready to stand on his own two feet. I told him he wouldn't mess it up . . . Oh, I said all sorts of things. I was arguing like a lawyer for a deserving client. In the end the old man agreed. He would assign the case to Vledder . . . if I didn't take off."

"What?"

"Yes, I'm supposed to hang around. Be on call, so to speak." He made an irritated gesture. "But I don't feel like doing that at all. So, in the end I just stopped talking and told him I needed time off. And now I want to get out of town for a few days. I want to go fishing."

For a long time she looked at him, searchingly, understanding. The irritated tone of voice had not escaped her. She knew him better than anyone, she knew all his virtues and all his faults. She knew all his moods and she was worried.

"May I come too?"

"Fishing?" he asked, astonished at the request.

"Yes, fishing."

He grinned. His face assumed an expression of boyish delight. A grinning DeKok was irresistible. He never knew how much she loved him at that moment.

"All right," he said, "if you want. Tomorrow we load everything into the old horseless carriage and we'll take off. I'll call Berends. He has a summer cottage somewhere near there. I'm sure he'll let us use it."

"And what about the dog?"

"Monty is coming, of course." He ruffled the dog's neck with a tender smile on his face. "There's plenty of room in the cottage. And it's a holiday for him, too. A change of trees will do him good." He rose from his chair, all energy. "Excellent," he said, "really excellent. I'm going to get my gear together."

She went to the kitchen. After a while she found him in the shed and persuaded him to come inside for some coffee. He sat at the kitchen table and watched her pour the coffee. How many cups had she poured for him over the years? It made him thoughtful. It was such an idle, almost silly thought. He tried to calculate it, but gave up ... thousands of cups ... tens of thousands of cups ... or more. He grinned to himself. An army of coffee cups, a canal full of coffee. Suddenly he looked at her, sharply.

"I never knew," he said with a hint of suspicion, "that you liked fishing. You never came with me before. You never wanted to go fishing."

She pretended not to hear him and filled her own cup, pushing the sugar jar closer to him.

"Come on, darling," he pressed. "I don't understand it. Why do you want to come? As far as I know you've never before held a fishing rod in your hands."

She poured cream in her coffee and slowly looked up, a playful smile on her lips.

53

"I've never," she said sweetly, "seen pikes waiting in line to be snared."

6

Vledder looked pale and there was a nervous tic on his cheek. He paced the large detective room with long steps, avoiding obstacles and persons without seeing them. Sometimes he sat down for a moment, but never for long. Then he would stand up to pace again. He was excited, restless and above all . . . unsure of himself. When DeKok was there it all seemed so easy, so simple and every step in the course of the investigation seemed to be so self-evident that he had often before wished to emerge from the shadow of his mentor and become independent.

Alex Delzen's murder had seemed like the perfect opportunity to prove his ability, show what he could do. Poisonings were the most difficult types of murders to solve — he knew that — and that had been one more reason to insist on going it alone. He would have the opportunity to establish his reputation as a detective for all time. In a way he had tricked DeKok into agreeing. He had said that he saw a possibility to unmask Delzen's killer. But it had not been the truth, it had been a bluff, overconfidence . . . self–delusion. He saw no clues, no possibilities. As a matter of fact, he did not have the faintest idea where to start.

He stopped in the middle of the room and sighed deeply. He was not getting any results by just doing nothing. *Hora Ruit . . .*

time passes. It would not be long, a few days at the most, and the Commissaris would want a progress report. And he had better be ready with something useful. After all, the old man was not exactly senile. No, he would not get away with vague excuses. He would have to have something concrete.

He scratched behind his ear, then he sighed again and made a decision. He would visit the students, the "Cluster". That would be his first step. After all ... he had to start somewhere.

* * *

"Alex Delzen ... murdered ... absurd." Emanuel Archibald Shepherd, graduate student in Sociology, looked at young Vledder with disbelief on his face and a supercilious, superior manner. "Murdered," he repeated in a mocking tone of voice. "You're serious?"

"Poisoned," confirmed Vledder seriously. Shepherd wrinkled his nose and grinned unpleasantly.

"My, my, poisoned you say?" It sounded both forced and incredulous. "A silly assumption ... surely?"

"Silly?"

Shepherd threw both arms in the air with a theatrical gesture.

"Of course," he said impatiently. "Silly ... thoroughly silly. Why would Alex Delzen be killed? Who would kill him? I mean, a murder pre-supposes a murderer ... am I right?"

"Correct," answered Vledder calmly. "You are correct. There are always two people involved in a murder. Cain slew Abel. It has been thus from the beginning." He paused and gave the student a deprecating smile. "Except in the old days ... in the old days, God would punish the perpetrators. But he doesn't do that any more. It's now *my* task to find Delzen's killer."

Shepherd did not respond at once. He gauged the expression on Vledder's face and seemed to estimate the level of intelligence.

"Is it," he started, hesitatingly, "is it possible . . . that a mistake has been made? *Murder* . . . it sounds so . . . so horrible. Does it have to be murder? I mean . . . aren't there any other possibilities?"

Vledder pushed his lower lip forward. Suddenly he looked a lot like DeKok.

"I'm afraid not," he said quietly. "The toxicological research was conclusive. Identifiable traces of poison have been found in the body. Investigations like that are carefully conducted," he added as if the student was in Grade School. He smiled broadly. "You do understand, don't you, that the police can't afford to be mistaken."

Shepherd had noticed the slight insult, the minute tweaking of his vanity, and abandoned his superior manners. He shook his head slowly.

"No, of course . . . I understand . . . I understand completely." He hesitated. "But forgive me, Inspector, it still seems so absurd. I find it hard to believe. I mean, who would gain by his death?" He shrugged his shoulders. "Nobody would gain by that, you can believe me, he was one of the nicest fellows in the house. Personally I liked him very much. I considered him a friend."

"Your friend?"

"Yes, my friend. And I'm proud to call him my friend."

"You were his friend," nodded Vledder. "Did he have any enemies?"

"Who? Alex?" Shepherd grinned and shook his head decisively. "No, not Alex. I told you . . . he was generally well liked. Everybody liked him. And with some justification, I might add. He was cheerful, friendly, intelligent . . . yes, extremely intelligent. Always helpful . . . nobody ever called upon him in vain. That's why . . . why it's almost unthinkable that somebody . . ." He paused, seemed to think of something. "Look," he continued, slowly, "if it had been suicide . . . if you had told me that Alex had killed himself . . . perhaps I could have understood." He seemed to consider. "But murder . . . no, never."

Vledder gave him a penetrating look.

"That doesn't sound very convincing," he said. "Why suicide, but not murder?"

Shepherd plucked nervously at a shirt-sleeve.

"That's a bit difficult to explain," he began.

"Try me," interrupted Vledder drily.

"Well, you see, the student world has its own atmosphere. It's different. Everybody is continually trying to convince everybody else about his, or her, point of view, is forever explaining their thoughts, feelings, experiences. Perhaps you're not aware of that, but there's a lot of conversation going on among students . . . regular debates, until well into the night." He paused. "Alex loved that. He was an excellent debater and he always participated to the fullest . . . sharp, energetic. Especially lately, when there was a lot of talk about . . ." He stopped and did not complete the sentence. Vledder waited several seconds.

"What were you going to say," he prompted.

Emanuel Archibald Shepherd grinned sheepishly.

"Now that I *do* think about it . . . lately murder has often been the topic of conversation."

The student rubbed his high forehead with the tips of his fingers. It was a typical gesture and he did it often. Subconsciously, especially when he was thinking, when he weighed his words. The automatic movement of the fingers seemed to form a stimulus and an accompaniment to his thought processes.

"Strange," he said pensively, "as recently as the night before Alex's death, murder was the topic of conversation." He stood up. He hunched his shoulders forward, as if sheltering from bad weather. He shivered and a tic developed on his pale face. "It's almost," he panted, "it's almost lugubrious."

"What do you mean?"

Shepherd did not answer at once. He walked over to the window, looked out and then turned, facing Vledder. His silhouette was darkly delineated against the strip of blue between the trees alongside the canal. His face was in shadow.

"It . . . eh, . . . it was rather a vehement debate . . . unusually vociferous, almost strident. Especially Kluffert and Delzen seemed to be going at each other tooth and nail. Ernst Kluffert was positively unable to reconcile his views with those of Delzen, who defended suicide."

"Delzen defended suicide? I thought the debate was about murder, homicide?"

"Of course, but suicide is, after all, a variant of homicide. The subject was therefore not out of order. In any case, Delzen, who led the debate, had introduced it himself."

"How?"

Shepherd made an annoyed, almost bored gesture. He was regaining some of his superior airs.

"Alex teased them into it. He declared that suicide, self–killing, could be morally supported under certain circumstances and was therefore not contrary to generally accepted mores and customs. He even went so far as to call suicide an act of moral courage."

"A bold statement," said Vledder, "but a bit beside the point, surely? Now that euthanasia is readily available, suicide is hardly an issue any more."

Shepherd smiled condescendingly.

"Perhaps, but if you know that Kluffert comes from a strictly religious background . . . then you'll also understand that he would never be able to accept Delzen's viewpoint. The same for euthanasia. It went directly against his character, his very being. He maintained and defended the Roman-Catholic point of view: Suicide is a mortal sin for which no absolution is possible. Kluffert argued heatedly with Delzen, furiously with a Christian, almost fanatical intolerance."

"*Christian* intolerance?" frowned Vledder.

"Did you," mocked Shepherd, "ever hear of the Inquisition? Persecutions, the stake, the witch trials, Crusades, Catholics against Protestant, Protestants against Catholics and each other, all of them against the Jews, or the Moslems, or whoever had the temerity to believe differently."

Vledder nodded slowly, more to dismiss the subject than to agree. The last thing he needed, or wanted, was a religious discussion. Vledder was of the firm opinion that neither religion, nor politics, was ever a fit subject for discussion between gentlemen. He certainly did not want to discuss it with the glib student. His only desire was to shed some light on the murder by poison.

"You said something about Kluffert?"

"Oh, yes," grinned Shepherd maliciously, "that worthy . . . he became red in the face . . . almost purple . . . and for a moment I thought he was going to attack Delzen physically when, I must say, after a masterly discourse, Delzen elevated death to, get this, *Man's best friend.*" He laughed again.

"What?"

"Yes, it was great, inspired. In his defence of suicide, Delzen pleaded for death."

Vledder frowned with incomprehension.

"Pleaded for death?"

"Yes, but not the way you think. He didn't ask for it. I mean pleading, like a lawyer. His closing arguments, so to speak. It was very impressive. You should have been there. It was typical Delzen in top form." He thought and then continued in a loud, declamatory voice. "Is life too much for you?" he said, obviously imitating Alex Delzen. "Go to him who soothes all pain. Are you tired and worried, go to him who offers eternal rest. Why subject yourself to a fruitless search for peace? Life has nothing to offer you. Why endure tortures any longer? Escape the terrible threats of nuclear weapons, war, famine and crime. Why tarry like a fool on this earth? There's nothing to find but toil, strife, sorrow and uncertainty. Believe me, only one can give you peace, only one can make you forget. He's so close. He's man's best friend and his name is Death."

A silence fell between them. The words of the student seemed to linger in the air, echoed from the walls. They confused Vledder, but also angered him.

"That's pure rubbish," he said. "That's how Jonestown happened. That's how the tragedy in Waco, Texas happened. That's how cult leaders lead their followers to slaughter. This . . . this deification of death. It's obscene, macabre." He grinned without mirth at his own weakness for getting involved in a debate, after all, despite his best intentions. "The frightening thing is," he added, "that it sounds so convincing."

"Convincing . . . exactly," nodded Shepherd. "It was. That's exactly the right word. It sounded convincing, then . . . that night . . . the night before he died." He sighed. "It sounded so convincing that we all fell silent. We were impressed. Even Kluffert did not say another thing. There was a suffocating atmosphere . . . something oppressive. Everybody felt it. You understand, I was only paraphrasing as best I could. But it seemed to everybody that Delzen had not only been pleading for his friend, Death, but also for himself."

They remained silent for several minutes after that. Vledder bit his lip and thought about what he had heard. Tried to imagine Delzen as he had stood there, orating, defending death . . . death so close.

"I see what you mean," he said finally. "In retrospect it *does* seem that Alex Delzen had already planned suicide and that he excused himself in advance."

"Yes," sighed Shepherd, "something like that." He looked glum and shrugged his shoulders. "Of course, it's impossible to determine if it was indeed the case, but, as you say, in retrospect . . . I mean, his sudden death, the very next day . . ." He hesitated. "You'll have to admit . . . it's remarkable, don't you think?"

"Remarkable," repeated Vledder softly while his quick mind considered the possibilities. Suicide was not ruled out. As a matter of fact, suicide had become a distinct possibility. But only a possibility.

Emanuel Archibald Shepherd moved away from the window. His face emerged from the shadows. Slowly he went around Vledder and sat down on the edge of his bed. The sharp lines of his face were now clearly visible, the small nose with the wide nostrils, the sunken, pale-blue eyes. He lowered his head.

"Poor Alex," he sighed, "poor, poor Alex . . . my friend." It sounded sad and his eyes were moist with tears. "Who could have ever imagined it? It's terrible." He made a helpless gesture. "More than terrible. Just like that, without a ripple, somebody you knew, somebody from your immediate circle . . . that somebody can be so tormented as to be capable of the ultimate deed, of killing himself."

Vledder rose from his chair, with the back of his mind he wondered if he was seeing real tears, or not.

"Yes," he agreed, "you're right. It's terrible." He looked down from his height and observed the bowed head, the dishevelled hair.

For a long time Vledder stood there, undecided. He was trying to think what DeKok would do under the same circumstances. No doubt he would have had a final question. The old sleuth always kept something in reserve ... a friendly *coup de grace* that forced one to think.

But Vledder could not think of anything. He turned around, murmured a farewell and abruptly left the room. In the corridor he bumped into a young man who had obviously been listening at Shepherd's door. It was Ernst Kluffert.

7

DeKok drove his old car, an early model VW Beetle, along the curiously named Rokin, passed the traffic lights on the Dam and approached Prince Henry Quay via the Damrak. It was just past nine o'clock and the morning rush hour had largely dissipated. They passed the Criers Tower, so called because the wives and sweethearts of sailors in the days of sail used to gather at its base to wave a last farewell to their men, departing for voyages of years and sometimes forever.

DeKok turned left and increased the speed slightly. Mrs. DeKok, seated next to him, paid no attention to his driving. Although DeKok was probably the worst driver in Amsterdam, if not in the Netherlands, she had a touching, unshakable faith in his abilities. A faith that was shared by the boxer on the back seat, dozing lightly, its head between its paws.

The lights for the long Harbor Tunnel were green. Just before the entrance of the tunnel the side of the road was crowded with hitch-hikers holding up crudely made cardboard signs announcing their desired destinations.

"Horn," read DeKok. "Harlingen, Leeuwarden, Haarlem, Volendam." He turned to his wife. "I often wonder," he commented, "why there is a Harlingen in Texas and a Harlem in New York."

"How so?"

"Well, in Holland Harlingen is in the north, in Friesland, and Haarlem is in the West, on the coast. But in the States Harlingen is in the far south and Harlem is almost on the Canadian border."

"Really, Jurriaan, you have the oddest thoughts. It's a good thing there are no Americans in the car. The idea . . . implying that New York City is a Canadian border town."

Suddenly, in the middle of a wide curve, DeKok slammed on the brakes. It happened so suddenly that Monty slipped off the back seat in a tangle of legs and offended dignity and Mrs. DeKok almost banged her head on the windshield.

"What happened?" she asked, concern in her voice.

"Barsingerhorn," answered DeKok.

"What Barsingerhorn?"

DeKok turned toward her.

"A hitch-hiker. Didn't you see him? A hitch-hiker with a sign for Barsingerhorn."

"Surely you don't want to pick somebody up?" she questioned. "You never take hitch-hikers." She refrained from telling him that it was because DeKok preferred to restrict knowledge of his limited driving skills to herself and, occasionally, Vledder. DeKok had no illusions on that score.

"This one," smiled DeKok, "this one we'll take along." He stepped out of the car and pulled the front-seat forward in an inviting gesture. About five hitch-hikers came running.

"Barsingerhorn," called DeKok.

All but one slowed their pace and drifted back to the side of the road. A young man in a dark sweat-shirt and jeans came closer. He wore a thin, flaxen beard which did not conceal the lines of a weak chin. Clear blue eyes flickered behind glasses set in a metal frame. The unusually clear eyes studied DeKok.

"You have room?"

66

"Next to the dog," waved DeKok, "if you have no objections."

"No problem at all," answered the young man, shaking his head. "Dogs are good company."

"Where's your luggage?"

The young man pointed at a canvas bag on his shoulder.

"This is it." He crawled into the back seat. "Other than that I only carry some spiritual baggage. But that doesn't take any space," he added, smiling.

DeKok did not react, he locked the front-seat back in place, wriggled himself behind the wheel, started up and entered the tunnel. The boxer on the back seat placed a heavy paw on the young man's thigh by way of greeting. The young man scrunched a little farther into the corner, giving the dog room.

For a long time nobody spoke. Mrs. DeKok stared through the windshield, a bit withdrawn. She did not care much for the company of strangers. It made her restless and undermined her self-confidence.

North of Amsterdam DeKok turned left again and drove in the direction of Purmerend. Purmerend is famous in Holland for a number of reasons. It is situated between the former Beemster and Purmer lakes. These two lakes are part of the first five lakes drained by the legendary Jan Adriaenz Leeghwater and formed a decisive turning point in Holland's continual battle against the sea. The Purmer was also the first lake to be drained entirely by windmills with a movable cap, to which the wings were attached, and an outside winding gear. Until that time mills had a fixed cap, requiring them to be stopped when the wind changed, then turning the entire structure into the wind before pumping could be resumed. The new mills allowed for wind changes without having to interrupt the vital pumping process. The work on the Purmer was completed in 1631 and yielded more than 12,000 acres of new land. Work on the five lakes commenced in 1597 with the construction of dikes around the lakes and almost 200 windmills were specifically built for the project to pump the water into the surrounding canals and from there to the sea. Altogether Leeghwater created more than 250,000 acres for the Netherlands in his lifetime and laid the foundation for later, more ambitious projects. The surface of the former lakes, called "polders", is an average of twelve feet below see level, only protected by sand dunes and the 17th Century dikes.

All this went through DeKok's mind as he navigated the narrow road on top of the dike. Every once in a while he would glance into the rear-view mirror and look at the hitch-hiker. He wondered when the young man would start the offensive.

They were long past the small town of Purmerend when the young man leaned forward.

"It's very kind of you to pick me up," he said in a soft voice.

"I never pick up hitch-hikers," snorted DeKok brusquely.

"But . . . then why me?" wondered the young man.

"Because," grinned DeKok, "you want to go to Barsinger-horn." He glance into the rear-view mirror. "That's your destination, isn't it . . . Barsingerhorn?"

"That's what it said on my sign."

"Exactly," nodded DeKok with satisfaction. "That's what it said on your sign. And that's why I don't believe a word of it. I bet you have no idea where Barsingerhorn is."

"I don't understand," frowned the young man.

DeKok gestured.

"If you really had wanted to go to Barsingerhorn, you wouldn't have put it on your sign. You would have used the name of a nearby, larger town. Alkmaar, for instance. Because, after all, who has ever heard of Barsingerhorn . . . a hole in the wall, less than a thousand people." He paused and took a deep breath. "Let me tell you something, young man, you gambled on my curiosity. Somebody told you I was going to Barsingerhorn."

The young man sank back into the small space of the back seat.

"You're right. The sign was a trick to make you stop. You've seen through me rather quickly." He smiled faintly. "But then ... that was to be expected from a sleuth with your reputation."

Mrs. DeKok turned abruptly.

"You know my husband?" She sounded hostile.

"Yes," sighed the young man. "DeKok with ... kay-oh-kay, Detective-Inspector, Homicide ... attached to the old, renowned police station in Warmoes Street. Triumphant conqueror of many murder cases." He hesitated momentarily. "And now in flight."

"Flight?"

"Yes, in flight. Fleeing from the scene of a possible failure."

Mrs. DeKok blushed attractively, but it was her equivalent of getting red with anger.

"My husband did not take flight," she answered sharply. "He flees from nobody or nothing. He has voluntarily made room for Vledder, a young Inspector who deserves a chance."

The young man grimaced.

"That sounds very noble, but it's just an excuse ... a weak excuse at that. The truth is that your husband is afraid to tackle the problem. He's afraid of the combined intelligence of the students."

Mrs. DeKok's face became hard. She stared through the windshield and her light-green eyes filled with anger. If looks could have killed, the young man would have been a small heap of smoldering embers.

"You ... you," she stammered with fury, "you don't understand a thing. My husband ..."

DeKok placed a soothing hand on her knee.

"Don't get excited, my dear," he said softly in a compelling tone of voice. "Our young friend isn't serious. It's a new kind of psychological joke." Again he glanced into the rear-view mirror, caught the young man's eyes. "Isn't that so, Mr. .... eh?"

The young man attempted to make a bow, but the cramped quarters in the back of the VW defeated his attempts.

"Duyn," he said. "Rudolph Hans Duyn."

"Excellent," nodded DeKok. "Duyn, Rudolph Hans. After your magnificent performance as a hitch-hiker for Barsingerhorn, this second, provocative act is only a clear ... I should say a logical consequence."

He slowed down and steered for the side of the narrow road. They were on a long, lonely road which bisected the polder almost at right angles. The outline of a village shimmered in the distance. DeKok turned off the ignition switch. There was a friendly look on his face.

"Clarity," he smiled, "is the rallying-cry of youth. Clarity and truth. Why don't you tell me straight out what's on your liver. Without all this beating around the bush."

Duyn looked evenly at DeKok.

"I want you to return to Amsterdam and take charge of the Delzen case."

"Why?"

The young man sighed as if the troubles of the world rested on his shoulders.

"Because the murderer *must* be found." He leaned forward, eagerly. "You're the only one, Mr. DeKok, who has the faintest hope of unmasking Alex Delzen's killer." He spoke hastily, nervously. "When I heard you had gone on leave and had handed over the case to Inspector Vledder, I tried to contact you at once. Somebody told me you were going to Barsingerhorn."

"And you decided to become the lone hitch-hiker for that destination."

"Please understand, Mr. DeKok, I don't doubt the abilities of Inspector Vledder. He's probably quite competent in a way. But this is not a routine sort of case."

DeKok shook his head.

"No murder is *routine*," he said.

Duyn blushed at the implied reprimand.

"You know very well what I mean," he explained passionately. "The murder of Alex Delzen requires more than a routine investigation. It's not at all an open-and-shut case." He removed his glasses, wiped them with a slip of his sweat-shirt. "The usual motives are not part of the equation," he added.

"What?" asked DeKok with well-feigned surprise. "No love, hate, envy or jealousy?"

"And no passion or emotion," added Duyn.

"An emotionless killing?"

"Exactly, an emotionless killing . . . cool, calm, calculated and without a recognizable motive."

"You're well informed," mused DeKok. "Extremely well informed. I'd be tempted to say that you are as well informed as the murderer."

"You're drawing the wrong conclusion," answered Duyn sharply. "I didn't kill Alex . . . Alex Delzen was my friend."

A silence fell and DeKok turned slowly and with some difficulty in the cramped seat of the VW to look full in the face of the young man.

"Alex Delzen." said DeKok dully, "was poisoned. He must have trusted his killer."

"You're trying to say it's easy to administer poison to someone?"

"It wouldn't be hard," sighed DeKok, ". . . among friends."

Duyn's eyes widened, his nostrils trembled. He grabbed DeKok by a shoulder and roughly pulled him closer.

"I didn't kill Alex," he yelled wildly. The sound seemed three times as loud in the small car. "You think I would ask you to handle the case if I were guilty? You think I'm crazy?"

DeKok pushed the hand from his shoulder.

"Some murderers," he answered calmly, "suffer from a superiority complex. They have an unshakable faith in their own infallibility. And some . . . *want* to be discovered." he smiled faintly. "Tell me, Mr. Duyn, in which category should we place you?"

The young man paled, the red of excitement drained from his face. Tiredly he fell back into the seat.

"I don't belong in one of your categories," he whispered. "You're mistaken." He licked his lips. "I'm a member of the Dispute."

"*Hora Ruit?*"

"Yes, *Disputa Hora Ruit*, we like the old word. I have a room in the attic. Not exactly comfortable, but it serves the purpose." He paused, seemed to gather his thoughts. "From your point of view," he resumed, "I'm a reasonable suspect . . . you're right, as far as that goes. I *could* be Alex's killer. I certainly have had plenty of opportunity, I'm well aware of that." He smiled at DeKok. "I study Criminology. I'm interested in crime."

"Therefore your analysis of the motives . . ."

"Yes, and my appeal to you. I know about your reputation and I had hoped you would be in charge of the case. You see, I've expected Alex's murder for some time . . . I almost knew it was going to happen. Don't ask me for concrete facts, or proof. I don't have them. It was more a feeling . . . a strange, unreasonable feeling. Call it intuition, if you like. I've discussed it several times with Alex."

DeKok's eyebrows rippled. Since he had turned again to the front, the only possible witnesses were a mother duck and seven ducklings who crossed the road just in front of the car.

Mrs. DeKok's attention had been drawn by the movement of the ducks and Duyn was staring at the floor of the car. It was too bad, because it was a magnificent ripple and the ducks did not appreciate it at all, in fact, they hardly gave the car a second glance. The sight of the ducks touched DeKok, and his eyebrows subsided. Then, remembering Duyn's last statement, he asked:

"You talked with him about his murder?"

"Yes, about my feelings."

"And what was his response?"

"Alex just laughed. He thought it was a crazy idea. As a clairvoyant, he said, I'd starve to death, or something to that effect. He advised me to always predict happy things."

"So, Alex thought it was ludicrous that anyone would want to kill him?"

"Yes, preposterous was the word he used. When I insisted and told him that my feelings were based on reality, that I couldn't get rid of the idea, he challenged me to name someone who would want to kill him."

"And?"

"What?"

"Did you name his murderer?" asked DeKok impatiently.

Duyn looked dejected.

"One shouldn't make unfounded accusations," he said softly.

"But that didn't stop you from scaring Delzen with your message of doom."

"Alex was my friend," retorted Duyn sharply. "I wanted to warn him. I wanted to make him understand what I felt, suspected. All those people that adored him, admired him, but who in fact were filled with . . ."

DeKok cocked his head at the rear-view mirror.

". . . Hate, envy?" he queried.

The student clapped both hands to his face.

73

"No, that isn't it at all," he exclaimed. "Oh, hell, how can I make it clear to you? Alex Delzen was a threat to the others in the dis . . ., the Cluster, because of his intelligence, his natural superiority, his special qualities. Not a threat in the usual sense of the word, you see, but . . ." He paused, shook his head in despair. "Alex Delzen," he resumed, calmer, "was a dominating personality. He so much dominated the others with his presence that sometimes there just wasn't any room for them . . . they lost themselves . . . their identity . . . their personality."

"And what about you.

"I was happy to have my attic room."

They remained silent. Mrs. DeKok stared fixedly out of the windshield, an angry, disturbed look in her eyes. Duyn again stared at the floor of the car and the dog closed its eyes and went back to sleep. DeKok watched the clouds chase each other over the low landscape. Soon the first raindrops fell and he switched on the engine and then the wipers. Suddenly he engaged the gears and made a clumsy U-turn on the narrow road.

"You're going back?" asked Duyn.

"No, I'm taking you back to Purmerend. You can get a train back to Amsterdam from there. I take it you have enough money with you?"

"Yes, I do."

"In Amsterdam you can contact my colleague, Vledder. Believe me, he's an extremely capable detective."

"I can't change your mind?"

"No."

"Then," said Duyn, a determined look on his face, "I'll find Alex's killer myself." It sounded like a challenge.

DeKok merely nodded.

"Everybody is entitled to serve the Law," said DeKok with an expressionless face. But there was a certain emphasis on the last word and there was no question that DeKok pronounced the word with a capital letter.

Mrs. DeKok smiled, strangely reassured.

8

They drove away from the small railroad station in Purmerend. Mrs. DeKok turned in her seat and watched the lonely figure of Duyn recede into the distance, until they turned a corner. Then she straightened out and looked at her husband.

"A strange boy," she said vaguely.

"Who, Duyn?" asked DeKok, his attention on the road.

"Yes, of course. Why should he insist that you handle the case?"

DeKok shrugged his shoulders which created a noticeable wavering in the path of the automobile.

"Perhaps he feels responsible," he said.

"For the murder?"

"More or less," nodded DeKok.

She looked at him with a confounded look on her face.

"I don't understand you."

"A lot of murders are committed in people's imagination," said DeKok with an unhappy tone in his voice. "It's a good thing that few people actually convert their wishes into deeds." He paused, slowed down, peered at a traffic sign and proceeded, the underpowered engine pinging in the wrong gear. "I can very well imagine," he reasoned, "that there must have been several times in the past that Duyn wished Delzen's death . . . the thought of murder cannot have been a stranger to him. *I wish you were dead* is not just a saying, it's often a sincere wish."

"And now that Alex Delzen has really been killed," nodded Mrs. DeKok, "he feels responsible, guilty . . . at the very least it's on his conscience and he wants the murderer punished."

"That's about it," agreed DeKok. "And there may be others who feel the same way, because they had the same wishes at times. That little group of students, that . . . eh, that Cluster at the Brewers Canal seems to me to be a powder–keg, full of tension, ready to explode. I only hope . . ."

Mrs. DeKok interrupted suddenly.

"You're going the wrong way."

"What!?"

"Barsingerhorn . . . turn right here."

* * *

Vledder had his ubiquitous notebook in one hand, a pencil poised in the other.

"John Gelder?"

"Yes."

"You live on this floor?"

"Together with Haverman."

"You're studying . . .?"

"Biology."

"You knew Delzen?"

"Of course, very well."

"You know he was murdered?"

Gelder gave the young Inspector a condescending smile.

"Delzen has passed on . . . or so I heard."

Vledder gave him a searching look.

"You don't believe he's been murdered?"

78

"Who could have done it," Gelder answered, shaking his head, a tone of disbelief in his voice. "Somebody from here? A member of the Cluster?"

"Perhaps."

"We are civilized people."

"That's hardly a guarantee," grinned Vledder.

"You know very well what I mean." The student gestured impatiently. "Of course there were disagreements. Show me a community, any community, that does not have differences of opinion . . . But murder . . . no . . . unthinkable."

Vledder looked at the student, observed the solid, square body, the lank hair, the beady eyes behind horn-rimmed glasses.

"Delzen died because of parathion."

"An insecticide," nodded Gelder. "It's just like Alex to use parathion," he added tonelessly.

Vledder showed his astonishment.

"You think Delzen took the parathion himself?"

"Of course," Gelder nodded vigorously. "Of course Alex committed suicide . . . that's rather obvious, I should think."

"How's that?"

Gelder sighed tiredly, as if exasperated by so much incomprehension.

"Alex Delzen was an opponent of the use of insecticides. He . . . and with him many others . . . was of the opinion that the excessive use of insecticides, of chemicals, has destroyed the balance of nature, has ruined the environment and is the primary cause for imminent, racial suicide. Therefore, you see, Alex's suicide, using parathion, was a symbolic protest."

"You want me to believe," asked Vledder sarcastically, "that Delzen had an ethical, an idealistic motive for committing suicide?"

Gelder reacted sharply. He leaned forward. His eyes sparkled.

"Exactly. Delzen was a man of deeds. He abhorred the endless talk, talk, talk of politicians. Delzen was actively involved in fighting for a better world . . . a biosphere wherein it would be possible for mankind, animals and plants to live harmoniously. The co-existence of all nature. Delzen believed in that." He looked up at Vledder. "Is it too far fetched to accept that someone should be willing to die for his ideals?"

Vledder rubbed his face with a flat hand. The emotional diatribe of the student had taken him slightly aback.

"The effect of his death was minute," Vledder said softly. "Delzen died alone and lonely in a drunk cell. Not exactly an heroic death."

"That is indeed sad," agreed Gelder. "But we, the young people of today, tomorrow's future, we know why he died and we will carry on his work, pursue his objectives. Alex Delzen did not die in vain." It sounded high-minded, lofty and just a little pathetic.

Vledder studied Gelder for some time. He looked at the expression on the face and wondered if the man believed his own words, or if the young biologist had just uttered a bitter joke. Slowly he closed his notebook, stood up and left the room. He did not bother with a farewell.

* * *

Tanned, the after-glow of the sun still tingling on his skin and with warmth in his heart, DeKok returned after five full days of leave. A leave that had been single-mindedly devoted to the pleasures of fishing. The short vacation had done him a world of good and he stepped into the large detective room with a happy smile on his face and a cheerful greeting for everybody, including a few recently arrested miscreants, hand-cuffed to

80

their chairs while the arresting detectives completed the inevitable paperwork.

He stopped by Bert Berends' desk and thanked him heartily for the use of the cottage. But he also jovially called him the biggest liar of all time . . . a blot on the unsullied escutcheon of the Amsterdam detective corps.

"Pikes lined up in a row," he said derisively. "Taking numbers! I didn't see one single solitary pike. All I caught in that dirty, forgotten stretch of ditch water were some frogs. That was all." He paused, grinned to himself. "Be sure to let me know next time when you have a special spot for fishing. At least I'll know where *not* to waste my time."

Berends laughed out loud, not in the least offended.

"The bad carpenter always blames his tools," said Berends. "You just don't know how to fish, that's your problem. You might be some sort of detective, I won't make a judgement on that. You've been lucky a few times. But that only involves catching people. But when it comes to fish, especially pike, they're a lot smarter than people and you have to know what you're doing. You must think like a fish." He looked at DeKok, a pitying smirk on his face. "But when I give you a spot, my very own secret spot, where the pike are so crowded they have seriously been thinking about putting in highrise apartments, when it that special spot, I say, when you can't even manage to hook . . ."

DeKok raised his hands in protest. If Berends was allowed to get up a full head of steam about fishing, he could be there into the next day.

"Stop already," he laughed. "Keep it for tomorrow. But do tell me, please, where I can find young Vledder, my invaluable side-kick and fellow sleuth. I'm curious to see how he's making out. Has he arrested anyone yet?"

The expression on Berends' face grew somber.

"I'm afraid he's not doing at all well."

"Why do you say that?"

"You can see it," shrugged Berends. "The boy walks around with the face of a centipede with corns. You know what I mean. No smiles, no jokes. Too serious. A bad sign, if you ask me. If once you lose your sense of humor in our kind of work, you next lose your humanity. Isn't that so?"

DeKok nodded thoughtfully. He had often said the same thing himself.

"He won't take advice, either, or ask for help," sighed Berends. "I, myself, have asked him several times if I could help, do anything for him."

"And?'

"First he looked at me if I was from another world and then he barked that he didn't need any help, could handle it himself. Well . . . what else can a body do?"

"Well," answered DeKok, "at the very least I want to say 'hello'. Where can I find him?"

"In the interrogation room." Berends waved in that direction. "He's been sitting there by himself all day. Yesterday, too. I think he's working on a report, but I tell you, it's a strange thing to see him abandon his computer. He's got an old portable typewriter in there with him."

"Thanks."

Hands stuffed deep in his trouser pockets, DeKok ambled over into the direction of the interrogation rooms. He was slightly upset to learn that his pupil, his friend, was apparently in difficulty so soon after he had been given the opportunity to work on his own. He understood how Vledder must feel. It was a long time ago, but he had not forgotten his own salad days. He stopped in front of the door to the small room and listened. He heard the rattling of a typewriter, almost as fast as Vledder was usually able to bang away on his computer key-board. He forced a friendly smile on his face and stepped inside.

"Hello," he called cheerfully. "How are things?"

Vledder's fingers seemed to freeze in position over the keys of the ancient portable. Slowly he looked up to encounter the familiar face of his old mentor. Suddenly, in a flash, he realized how much he loved the old man. He was like a second father. The somber expression on his face cleared up and a happy smile broke through. Even as he smiled, a deep sigh escaped his lips.

"I'm happy to see you're back, DeKok," said Vledder with genuine sincerity. "Believe me, I'm happy to see you back."

9

"And who told you *that* fairy-tale?"

Vledder reacted sharply and defensively.

"It's not a fairy-tale," he exclaimed, indignation in his voice. "Just about all the members of the Cluster are convinced that Delzen committed suicide."

"Why?"

"Because ..." Vledder gestured helplessly. "Because ... the students consider the suicide of Delzen acceptable ... under certain circumstances. He, himself, had stated that many times and you should know that Delzen was in the habit of glorifying death."

"There are people," grimaced DeKok, "who long fervently for Heaven. But that doesn't mean they want to die." He looked probingly at his young friend, colleague and partner. "Do you have anything at all? Anything concrete? I mean, do you have anything that clearly points the way to suicide?"

"No, I don't," answered Vledder, shaking his head. "But there are also no indications that point to murder. There is no recognizable motive. Nobody had anything to gain from Delzen's death."

"Aha," grinned DeKok. "No motive for murder, ergo, it's suicide. Q.E.D." he added mockingly.

"What?"

"*Quod Erat Demonstrandum*, Latin for which was to be shown, or in a police context: As is to be proved."

Vledder shrugged his shoulders, spread his arms wide.

"What else can I do. I'm drafting my report on that basis."

"Why here? Your computer broke down?"

"Well ..."

"I see, you don't really believe it yourself, do you?"

"No," answered Vledder. "Personally ... you're right, I don't believe it. I don't believe it at all. It just doesn't compute. And that's exactly the trouble. I've been racking my brain for almost a week and I don't even see a glimmer of a solution. I just can't figure it out. It's not ... not logical, it doesn't fit ... neither one, or the other."

"Well, one or the other is right. He either killed himself and then we should be able to prove it, or he *was* killed and we should be able to prove that as well. What do the students say about it?"

Vledder sighed.

"The students in the house, the members of the Cluster, reject all suggestions of murder out of hand. It's totally unacceptable to them. Suicide, as far as they are concerned, is the only possibility. One of them, Gelder, even suggested that Delzen killed himself for idealistic purposes ... something like those Buddhist monks who burned themselves to death. He saw a symbolic significance in the death by parathion ... a protest against the use of insecticides."

"Did you find the poison?"

"No."

"You did *not* find the poison?" DeKok was astonished and it showed in his face and could be detected in the sound of his voice.

"No." Vledder shook his head wearily. "The Technical Squad, the forensic experts, myself ... we went over the house with a fine tooth-comb. But there was no parathion, or any other kind of poison, to be discovered. Nobody from the Cluster knew anything about poison. And yet . . . Delzen *must* have ingested the poison in that house on the Brewers Canal."

"You're sure of that?"

"Oh, yes," said Vledder with conviction. "I double checked with Dr. Eskes. He was quite certain that the poison could not have been in Delzen's system for more than twenty-four hours. That was the limit, he said."

"And?"

"It was a simple matter to establish that Delzen had not left the house for at least twenty-four hours before he was picked up on the Damrak."

"And what time did he leave?"

"About half past seven. He left the house about half an hour before he was noticed by Brink and Vries."

DeKok rubbed the bridge of his nose with a little finger.

"Was there any alcohol in the house?"

"Not a drop." Vledder shook his head vehemently. He smiled. "I know what you're after. How did Alex get the alcohol in his blood stream?"

"Exactly."

"I checked on that. I checked every bar between the Brewers Canal and the Damrak."

"Well," prompted DeKok.

"There are a lot of them, but I lucked out with number eight. You know it, I'm sure: *The Thirsty Stag*. I showed the barkeeper Delzen's photo and he recognized him immediately. Delzen went there often, as a matter of fact. On the night in question he stopped by a little after half past seven. Apparently he looked like sh . . . looked terrible," he corrected hastily. Vledder knew DeKok's opinion about off-color words. "He looked gray and he said he didn't feel well. According to the barkeeper, he thought

87

he had the flu, or something. In any case, Delzen asked for a couple of cognacs and downed them quickly, one after the other. Then he had a third one and left almost immediately thereafter. The barkeeper advised him to go home, to go to bed, but Delzen didn't want to hear about it. He couldn't do that, he said, he had an appointment."

DeKok nodded pensively.

"And he went into the bar by himself and left by himself?"

"Yes."

"He didn't feel right?"

"No."

"Well," said DeKok slowly, "negative information is also information. At least we can eliminate the possibility that he ingested the poison with the alcohol. At the time Delzen ordered his first cognac, the poison was already spreading through his system." He stared at Vledder, then he asked: "According to the barkeeper, Delzen drank three drinks in quick succession?"

"Yes."

"And he felt so bad that he diagnosed himself as having the flu, or something?"

"Yes."

"So, Delzen took the cognac for . . . medicinal purposes."

Vledder nodded, unsure of himself.

"Yes," he said, surprised. "Surely that's not unusual, is it? It sounds normal to me."

"Yes," agreed DeKok, who had long since been converted to a belief in the medicinal purposes of cognac, his favorite beverage. "It's the normal thing to do and we can draw another conclusion from that."

"A conclusion?"

"An important conclusion. You see, Alex Delzen *did not know* he had been poisoned."

"What!?"

88

"Think about it. Alex Delzen was not aware of the danger. He thought in terms of a severe flu, or something similar. Therefore he took some cognac ... as medicine. He never thought about poison."

Vledder stared at him, wide-eyed and with a look of admiration on his face.

"Dammit," he panted. "You're right. I never thought about that. But of course, now that you point it out, it's logical ... if Delzen had committed suicide, if he had taken the poison himself, he would have *known* it wasn't the flu."

DeKok smiled.

"And what follows then?"

"If he didn't take the parathion himself," grinned Vledder, "he didn't die of suicide but ..."

"... as the result of murder," completed DeKok.

A silence fell between them. The figure of the dead student was almost a tangible presence in the room. His death had suddenly gained a new dimension ... an added person ... a suspect ... the murderer.

10

Vledder looked at his old friend and mentor with genuine admiration.

"You know, DeKok . . . when you're around it all seems so easy . . . so . . . so simple." He laughed cheerfully. "You know, I'm getting back my appetite for this case. You have no idea how low I felt. I truly was at wit's end . . . saw no hope."

DeKok gave him a chiding look.

"And then you figured . . . come, let's call it suicide," he was unable to keep a slight hint of derision out of his voice.

Vledder blushed. He had heard the gentle reprimand and knew it was deserved.

"Well, yes," he said apologetically, "but you shouldn't blame me, not really. You told me how difficult a poisoning can be and . . . I found out. After all," he added forthrightly, "I don't have your experience."

DeKok snorted but did not answer. He hunted through his pockets, found a stick of chewing gum, unwrapped it and placed the stick between his teeth. He dropped the wrapper on top of the draft pages of Vledder's report.

"I had to do *something*," said Vledder, remembering his boast that he could handle it and grateful to DeKok for not mentioning it.

"Let's forget it," smiled DeKok, aware of his partner's thoughts. "And while we're at it," he advised, "let's tear up that report you've been working on. Has anybody else seen it yet?"

"No," answered Vledder. "That's why I didn't do it on the computer. I was going to enter it, after I had the draft worked out."

"What about the Commissaris?"

"He's been asking for me, but I've managed to stay out of his way."

"Excellent, really excellent. Then nobody has to know."

"Thanks," answered Vledder in a small voice. "I admit I didn't do so well." He tore the last page out of the typewriter, stacked the sheets and proceeded to tear them into pieces. "Sometimes I wonder if I'll ever get anywhere."

DeKok laughed at him.

"Don't give up the ship," he admonished with a twinkle in his eye. "I'll see you as a Commissaris yet." He placed a fatherly hand on the young man's shoulder. "Just keep at it, you'll get there."

Vledder's face assumed a determined look.

"Dammit . . . sorry DeKok, but those . . . those *students* have been leading me down the garden path. Them and their theories about suicide. I'll . . . I'll . . ."

"You're going to do nothing of the kind," said DeKok calmly, shaking his head. "You've been acting like a bull in a china shop long enough. It's about time that we take matters in hand. To begin with . . . let's review what you have done so far. For instance, those two theater tickets . . . did you find out who Delzen was supposed to meet that day?"

"I don't know," shrugged Vledder. "Nobody could tell me. The general opinion was that it would probably have been a girl. Women liked Delzen. One of the students referred to him as a sexual genius."

"I suspect," grinned DeKok, "that it was probably more sexual than genius."

Vledder, too, was not immune to a grinning DeKok and he grinned in return.

"Well, I wouldn't know. I didn't know Delzen personally. Whatever it was, he seemed to have maintained extensive contacts with the opposite sex."

"What sort of women?"

"I never found out," sighed Vledder. "Of course I tried to find out. After all, it could have been a motive. But Delzen must have been of the school that maintains that a gentleman never tells. In other words, he did tell his fellow-students about his sexual adventures, but he never mentioned names."

"How very considerate of our Alex."

"Yes," nodded Vledder. "Overall I did not get a bad impression about Delzen. He was the oldest member of the Cluster and the *primus inter pares*. Reasonably intelligent and outstanding in most things . . . love . . . sports. He was respected by his fellow students, was very well liked . . . also he apparently had plenty of money. His parents are very rich."

"Envy?"

"In a way." Vledder dropped the last, tiny pieces of his aborted report in the trash can, along with DeKok's discarded gum wrapper. "At one time or another all the students, some more, some less, envied him. But, you see, I was unable to discover anything that could be termed 'hate', not by a long shot. They were very much upset about his death and they all seemed saddened by it . . . without exception."

"What about political activities?"

"The rumors surrounding his death died out almost immediately," grinned Vledder. "And so did the accusations. Good thing too, otherwise I wouldn't have been able to keep dodging the old man."

"All right," nodded DeKok, "but were there any *motives* in the political environment?"

"I didn't notice much about that," admitted Vledder. "I consciously avoided any mention of politics during the interrogations."

DeKok's eyebrows danced across his forehead. Vledder was mesmerized. He missed part of what DeKok said next and asked him to repeat it.

"I said," responded DeKok, "that Delzen was supposed to be one of the leaders among the students, among the various student organizations. The Cluster at the Brewers Canal was a sort of Headquarters for student activities."

Vledder lowered his head.

"I know . . . but I didn't notice anything. To be honest . . . I didn't pay all that much attention to it. I read in one of the papers that last Spring Delzen and some other students went to Berlin for some sort of Congress. But the subject never came up during the interrogations."

"Did Delzen have his own room, or did he share a room with someone else?"

"He had his own room. Every student in the house has his own room. Haverman and Gelder live on the second floor, Kluffert and Marle live on the next floor. Delzen and Shepherd shared the ground floor. There is a large kitchen and pantry in the walk-out basement for communal use.

"What about the attic?"

"What about the attic?" asked Vledder, surprised.

"Duyn lives there," explained DeKok.

"Who?"

"Student Duyn, Rudolph Hans Duyn, Undergraduate student in Criminology. I met him on the way to Barsingerhorn. He asked me to return to Amsterdam to investigate what he termed the Delzen case. He's convinced that Alex was murdered."

Vledder was obviously astonished.

"I never knew that a Duyn lived in the house. I was under the impression that the attic room was just in temporary use." He pulled out his notebook and consulted a page. "Duyn," he added, "Duyn is one of the students that went to Berlin with Delzen."

"What?"

"Yes, I remember the name from a newspaper article. Haverman was the other student."

DeKok stared into the distance.

"Delzen's murder did not come as a surprise to Duyn. He said he had seen it coming."

"He expected the murder? On what grounds?"

"Intuition."

Vledder snorted, reverting back to his usual opinion about feelings and intuition, especially as they applied to a murder case.

"Yes."

"Intuition," repeated Vledder with a deprecating gesture. "What use is intuition?" he paused, drummed his fingers on top of the table. "And yet," he said, hesitating, looking for the words. "It's strange . . . I've had a feeling . . . that something was about to happen . . . that within the Cluster something was ready to come to a head, to explode."

"What made you think that?"

"There was too much talk about murder."

"By whom?"

"The students . . . they had regular meetings and debates, usually in Delzen's room. They debated about death . . . and murder. As far as I've been able to gather, it was a frequent subject. Murder was discussed on the night before Delzen's death."

"Murder in debate," said DeKok, "murder in dispute . . . a nice title for a dissertation, or one of those books by that fellow Baantjer." He stood up and deposited a wad of chewing gum in the trash can. "It's remarkable," he went on, "how the subject of murder preoccupies people, fascinates them. People read about it, write about it, talk about it with an interest, a fervor that's almost . . . frightening. Why? Because a murderer hides within each and every one of us? Because we all know at least one person who, for whatever reason, we would gladly see disappear from this vale of tears? Usually it remains an unspoken wish. But sometimes, when the thought grows into a compulsion, a neuroses . . . when the mind is continually obsessed with thoughts of murder . . . when all restraints are abandoned and reduced to a simplistic formula of *to be or not to be*, then . . ."

Vledder interrupted with a loud laugh, disturbing DeKok's train of thought. He looked at the young Inspector with amazement.

"What's the matter with you?"

Vledder shook his head, still chuckling.

"Nobody asked you to write a dissertation on murder . . . you have to solve one."

DeKok looked puzzled.

"That," he said resignedly, "is what I was working on."

11

They walked across the Damrak toward the Dam. As usual, it was busy in the huge square. The colorful tones of dozens of languages and dialects formed an exotic background to the sights and sounds and smells of the heart of Amsterdam. A barrel organ played in front of the entrance to the Central Railroad Station. Beautiful women paraded in bright, light clothes past the full terraces and provided part of the sights. A wonderful free show for those who could appreciate it. The flags along the piers for the sight-seeing boats waved gaily in the breeze under a clear, blue sky. The smells were provided by the many restaurants and numerous stalls that served a variety of foods. An overpowering part of the smell was caused by Moshe, the Herring Man, who parked his cart near the Warmoes Street station and had a regular spot near the piers. From there he dispensed the so typical Dutch snack. Tourists would gape and shiver in wonder as the herring man deftly scaled a raw herring, divested it of head and intestines, whereupon the customer would just as deftly pick the cleaned herring by the tail, briefly slide it through the raw onions and then, with head bent far back, would let the fish slide down in two, maybe three bites, leaving only the tail. The Dutch consumed tons of the fish, each year.

Vledder and DeKok stopped at Moshe's cart and they indulged in three herrings each. DeKok could eat herring at any time of the day or night, but the bright sunny day made the esoteric snack twice as enjoyable. Vledder, although he certainly did not dislike the fish, joined him automatically. He was deep in thought.

As they proceeded on their way, DeKok pushed his faithful, little hat further back on his head and winked daringly at a young prostitute who was trying her luck away from the Red Light District. She nodded at him with the air of a duchess who had just noticed one of her peasants. DeKok smiled as her perfume engulfed them, driving away the last, lingering smell of the herring.

Vledder had not noticed any of this by-play. His face was serious and a deep crease marred the smooth outline of his forehead. The sights and sounds and smells that so stimulated DeKok time and again, were wasted on Vledder. He did not hear the many languages, was unaware of the barrel organ, had no eyes for the female beauty in the street, or on the terraces. He dodged tourists and other pedestrians without seeing them and had already forgotten the taste of the herrings and the crispy onions. He was thinking about murder.

"Say," he said suddenly. "I hope you're not planning to interrogate all those students again. It would make me look a bit foolish, don't you think? Besides . . . I think I've already asked them everything."

DeKok shrugged his shoulders, with difficulty tearing himself away from savoring his beloved city.

"It depends on what I hear from the *factotum*."

"The factotum?"

"Yes. Every self-respecting student society, or rooming house, or *dispute*, has a factotum, a servant, an odd-jobs man, a gofer . . . what the British call a 'man', as in 'my man'. He usually keeps the rooms clean, runs errands, stokes the boiler in winter . . . things like that. I don't think that this particular Cluster at the Brewers Canal is different. They seem to be organized along traditional lines. We'll have to check. Usually such a factotum lives nearby."

Vledder shook his head in despair.

"I never knew," he moped, "that there was such a person. A factotum . . . never heard of it."

"Now that we're moving in student circles," grinned DeKok, "you really should brush up on some of the language they use. Brush up your Latin . . . Didn't you have anything to do with that when you went to College?"

"No," said Vledder, "I lived at home and I had to work on the side. I just attended classes and had no time for all the social frills." He paused. "As a matter of fact, they mailed me my degree, because I had already joined the force. Besides . . . my degree is in History, you do a lot of private research for that. Also, I didn't go to one of the University towns, such as Amsterdam, Leiden, or Utrecht."

"You sound bitter," said DeKok, reflecting that one could work with a partner for years and still could learn something new about that person.

"No, not bitter. It just happened that way. Anyway," continued Vledder, changing the subject, "what can such a factotum tell us about Delzen's death?"

DeKok smiled.

"A lot . . . I hope. You see, often a factotum is also used as a sort of father-confessor. He's usually an older man and they entrust him with their little secrets, affairs . . . sometimes he carries notes between lovers . . . a *postilion d'amour*."

"All right," Vledder snorted, "father-confessor, I can understand that, but *postilion d'amour*! Really, that's so old–fashioned. Goodness, it makes me think of Cyrano de

Bergerac, or Myles Standish. Today we use the telephone, or the fax. More efficient."

DeKok was willing to be distracted.

"Cyrano I know, the one with the nose. But who's Myles Standish?"

"American colonist, apparently too ugly to dare ask the hand of Priscilla Mullins. Used John Alden as a *postilion d'amour*. Longfellow wrote a poem about it. He fought on Dutch soil, you know, for the British. Standish I mean, not Longfellow. That's probably how he met the Pilgrims. He sailed on the *Mayflower* as their military leader."

"I can see you studied history. I knew the Pilgrims lived in Holland for a while and had a church in Leiden. It's still there. Before they went to Leiden, they lived in Amsterdam, in the English Pilgrim Alley as it's now called. But I didn't know all that other stuff."

"Oh, well ..."

"But to get back to the subject," said DeKok, "don't think that romance has died. Telephone ... fax ..." DeKok made them sound like obscenities and in his mind they probably were. "You use those things for business ... not for love. Nossir, romance is still alive and even the most emancipated woman will be responsive to a romantic gesture. Believe me, love letters are still written, every day. Even young people do it." He gestured enthusiastically. "And what can be more romantic than a fiery love letter, delivered by special courier?" He looked at the disapproving face of his young partner. "Have you never been in love?" he asked.

Vledder did not answer. He was not about to reveal that he kept every letter that Celine, his fiancee, had ever written him. And he was sure Celine still had all of his.

* * *

100

"In love?" Old man Drager pursed his lips and bobbed his head up and down. "Oh, yes, young master Delzen was often in love. I would estimate at least twice a month."

"Rather frequently," laughed DeKok.

"What did you say?"

"Rather a lot."

The old man bobbed his head again. He leaned back in his rattan chair and sucked comfortable on a corn-cob pipe. It made an unpleasant, gurgling sound. The old chair creaked in protest.

"Ach," said the old man tolerantly, "he was a boy with a southern temperament, you understand. What do you expect, there was more sun in his bones than with us cold northerners. It wasn't his fault. What could he do about it?"

DeKok did not know.

Vledder joined the conversation.

"Did you ever," he asked, "deliver any love letters for him?"

Old Drager seemed to sink into reverie.

"Oh, my, yes. I delivered a letter for him."

"A love letter?"

"I think it was a love letter," nodded the old man.

"Where did you deliver the letter?"

"Do I have to answer that?"

"Yes, please."

"I . . . eh, I promised not to talk about it." The old man rubbed the inside of his wide collar with a nervous finger. "You see, it isn't all that pleasant for one of the other students."

"Not pleasant?"

"Yes, you see, the letter I delivered for master Delzen . . . was addressed to the sister of young master Kluffert."

"So?"

"You don't know that, of course," sighed the old man, "but Kluffert and Delzen weren't such good friends. Nossir, they sure

101

weren't. Young master Kluffert disliked master Delzen, yessir. He disliked master Delzen's easy-going ways with the ladies, you see. It irritated him greatly and if he had known that master Delzen had a relationship with one of his sisters . . . there would have been hell to pay and no pitch hot, yessir, that's a fact."

"In short," stated Vledder, "Delzen had an affair with Kluffert's sister?"

"You've got the right of it there, young sir."

"And Kluffert never found out?"

"I don't think so," shrugged the old man. "I would have most certainly heard about it, yessir, I would have heard about it. You see, young master Kluffert isn't the easiest of persons to get along with."

"How do you mean"

Drager grinned.

"There would have been a row, yessir, a row," he said with a certain amount of relish.

"Thank you," said Vledder curtly. He bit his lip and thought about what he had heard.

DeKok pushed his chair closer and presented a friendly face. He had observed carefully while Vledder asked his questions and he had noted every expression on the old man's face.

"Did you know *all* of Delzen's loves?"

The old man cackled disdainfully.

"All of master Delzen's loves . . . nossir, that would have been too much to ask. The young master didn't keep any secrets from me, it isn't that, you see, he told me plenty about his adventures. With quite some details in fact, yessir, with a lot of detail. As far as I knew he had no secrets from me, nossir, he didn't. But *all* his love affairs?" He cackled again. "Nossir, he must have lost track himself, from time to time. Yessir, he must have lost track."

"That many?"

"It was so bad," said the old man, shaking his head with a melancholy expression, "that it affected his health, yessir, he started to look bad, peaked, you know." He sucked once more at his pipe. "What's your opinion of today's young ladies, sir? What do you think about them? I mean, they demand a lot from a body, don't they? Yessir, they take it out of one, don't they?"

The old man was getting more garrulous by the minute. DeKok had difficulty maintaining a straight face.

"Yes," he admitted simply, "I guess you're right. I don't know much about it."

"Well, you take it from me, sir." The old man bobbed his head decisively. "Yessir, you take it from me. I see a lot and I hear a lot, yessir, I do."

"Among the students?"

The old man moved in his chair, found a more comfortable position, prepared to discourse at length.

"Generations, sir, I've taken care of generations of students. Yessir, I've done this work for years ... decades. Believe me, I know the troubles of youth, yessir, I know them. I know what they're thinking and hoping. Youth has always been exuberant, yessir, a bit loose I might say ... even in the good old days. But the way it is today, yessir, the way they carry on today ..." He paused with a meaningful look in his eyes. He shook his head and made soft tut-tut sounds. "No shame, sir, no shame at all, that's what's the trouble, yessir, no shame. They practically advertise their ... how shall I say it ... their needs, yessir, their needs ... they walk around with their needs for all to see. And the girls, you wouldn't believe, sir, the girls ..." He paused again and Vledder reflected that with DeKok's extensive experience in the Red Light District, there was little DeKok would not believe about women. "Take for instance," continued the old man, "take Ella Rosseling."

DeKok interrupted the stream of consciousness.

"Ella Rosseling?"

The old man gestured wildly.

"The woman, the lady I should say, yessir, the lady with whom master Delzen had a relationship for some time. You know ..."

DeKok interrupted again.

"I'm sorry," he said softly, apologetically. "I don't know a thing. The love affairs of Alex Delzen somehow slipped between the net of our investigations. Nobody could tell us anything about them. Therefore, you see, I'm so happy to learn that young master Delzen trusted you, yessir, I'm really happy about that. Isn't that so, Dick?" He glanced at Vledder.

Vledder swallowed.

"Yessir," he answered, "very happy indeed, yessir, happy." He hastily searched for a handkerchief. Something seemed to be choking him.

The old man took the flattery at face value and he pushed out his chest.

"Well, you see," he said proudly, "I'm almost a father to the young gentlemen. They often come to me for advise about things they don't dare discuss with their own parents, yessir, they don't discuss it."

"I understand completely," nodded DeKok seriously. "But let's return to Ella Rosseling. You were, I thought, about to tell us something about her?"

"Oh, yes, Ella Rosseling, that br ... eh, that woman." He shook his head in a disapproving way. "A whore, sir, if you ask me, no more than a prostitute." He grinned falsely. "She just didn't ask money for it, nossir, she didn't ask money."

"No money?"

"Well, actually, she didn't ask money from master Delzen. I don't know about the others. But she was crazy about master

104

Delzen, yessir, crazy. One time she made a scene, in the house, mind you, when she found out master Delzen saw other women, yessir, she made a scene."

"And that was the end of the relationship?"

The old man shook his head with vigor.

"She was in his room the day he died, yessir, the day he died."

"What!?"

"Yessir, on the day he died. Positively. I can prove it too."

Old man Drager stood up and shuffled to another room. Within seconds he came back and held up a soft, shiny black garment like a trophy. DeKok looked surprised. It was a soft, silk laced slip. A frivolous, showy piece of clothing.

"The young lady's underwear." The old man gestured with forced nonchalance. "I found it in the room, yessir, in the room."

"After his death?"

"Yessir, after his death, when I straightened out the room."

"Did you remove any other items from the room."

"No . . . no, other than that I didn't remove a thing, nossir, I didn't." It did not sound very convincing.

Inspector DeKok rubbed the material between his fingers with a thoughtful look on his face. After a while he looked at the old man.

"So this," he said guilelessly, "is Ella's slip?"

The old man nodded acquiescence.

"You're sure about that?"

"Yes."

"You couldn't be mistaken?"

"No."

"But surely, young Delzen must have received other ladies in his rooms. I mean, this slip could belong to one of the others."

"It's Ella Rosseling's underwear I tell you, yessir, it is." Drager sounded annoyed. His tone of voice was irritated and sharp. He seemed to have lost some of his loquaciousness

"Well," mused DeKok, "in that case I cannot help but wonder how you can be so sure? After all, a slip is rather an intimate piece of apparel. And I cannot believe that the young gentlemen invited you as a spectator when they received female visitors in their room. Now, did they, Mr. Drager?"

The long, tawny face of the old man was enriched by a deep blush. He moved nervously in his chair. DeKok watched him in silence.

"You knew when Delzen received ladies?"

The old man nodded almost imperceptibly.

"How?"

The adam's apple in the narrow, scrawny neck bobbed up and down. Drager's tongue flicked at his lips. He was obviously uncomfortable.

"Did Delzen tell you in advance?"

"No."

"Then, how did you know?"

Old Drager began to shake slightly. The fire in his pipe had long since gone out and the self-satisfied, smug mannerisms had disappeared. He suddenly looked old, very old and pitiful. DeKok felt compassion, but his eyes remained aimed at the old man like the turret of a gun emplacement, questioning, compelling.

"Well . . .?" urged DeKok.

With a deep sigh the old man rose from his chair. It was a labored, difficult movement, as if all strength had left his legs. His bony hand gripped the back of the chair for support. Slowly he turned and his hand reached for a pair of binoculars. It was an ancient instrument in a torn leather carrying case and a greasy strap. The old man took it from a nail in the wall and walked over to the window.

"Come see," he whispered.

DeKok came over to stand next to him. On the other side, in between the trees, he could see the windows of the Cluster at the Brewers Canal. The distance was not very far. The window of Delzen's bedroom was clearly visible.

DeKok took the binoculars from the old man. Although old, the instrument was of excellent quality and the scene across the canal seemed to leap at DeKok as he brought it to his eyes and adjusted the focus. His vision stroked along the facade, briefly brushed one of the ornate sculptures on the edge of the roof and steadied on the window of Delzen's bedroom. The binoculars allowed him to penetrate into the room. The interior was clearly visible, the gray wall-paper, a bookcase, a small table, the bed . . .

DeKok lowered the binoculars and looked at the old man with a soft, disapproving look in his eyes.

"Voyeur," he said, "second-hand thrills."

The old man lowered his head.

DeKok replaced the binoculars on the nail in the wall. The old man had sat down again and stared into the distance. He seemed deflated, the spirit was knocked out of him.

The atmosphere in the room reflected the feelings of the old man. There was a cheerless, claustrophobic feel to the room. The right setting for confidences had disappeared. Old Drager looked disinterested and just a little stubborn after the discovery of his vice. In fact, DeKok realized, it was useless to continue the interrogation under the present circumstances. There was no more to be gained from the old man at the moment. Suiting the action to his thoughts, DeKok prepared to leave, but was restrained by Vledder, who shook his head at his partner. Vledder had been thinking about what they had learned so far and a possibility had occurred to him.

"So," said Vledder, "Ella Rosseling visited Alex Delzen on the day of his death?'

The old man merely nodded.

"Did you see the visit through your binoculars?" asked Vledder unperturbed. "I mean, also the times before and after the bed scene?"

"From the beginning," sighed Drager. "I saw her come and I saw her go." He seemed unaware of the implied pun.

"Did you notice anything peculiar during the visit?"

"No," denied the old man, ". . . nothing. Except that they went to bed."

"I mean," insisted Vledder, "did they drink anything?"

Drager tried to remember, his gaze traveled toward the ceiling.

"Yes," he said after a long pause, "They drank something . . . coffee."

"How do you know that."

"I saw her leave the room and a few minutes later she came back with two cups. I figured she had made coffee."

"That quick?" Vledder was skeptical.

"Sure," nodded the old man. "There's instant coffee in the kitchen and a special faucet for boiling water. It don't take long, nossir, not long."

"What happened to the cups?"

"I washed them of course . . . yes, washed them."

"I was afraid of that," sighed Vledder.

DeKok smiled to himself. He could follow Vledder's train of thought as if it had been printed in front of his eyes. The poison could have been introduced via the coffee.

"Did you know Ella Rosseling?" asked DeKok.

The old man shrugged.

"Know . . . what is *know*. I talked to her a few times when she asked after master Delzen. She was sharp . . . touchy. Not a kitten to handle without gloves, nossir, she'd scratch."

"Could she have . . .?"

"You mean . . . her and master Delzen?"

"Yes."

Old Drager pressed his lips together. His tawny face assumed a determined, closed look.

"I don't want to accuse nobody," he said firmly, "but if she had known that master Delzen wanted to break it off with her for good, then . . ."

"Was Alex planning to break with her permanently?"

"He was going to tell her that day," nodded the old man. "He wanted to get rid of her. You see, he and Miss Kluffert had serious plans. He had tried before, yessir, he had tried."

"Tried what?"

"To get rid of Ella Rosseling, of course, but he was a bit afraid. She's a snake, sir." Fire came into his eyes. "If anybody has killed young master Delzen, it would have been *her*. She's capable of anything . . . yessir, anything."

"Even murder?" asked DeKok.

"Even murder," confirmed the old man.

12

Vledder looked over his notes.

"Could Ella Rosseling have killed Delzen?" he asked himself and then answered his own question: "It's possible . . . if she thought he wanted to break off the relationship."

DeKok sat down and placed his legs on the desk.

"A *crime passionnel*," he said. "Hell hath no fury like a woman scorned."

"Why not," persisted Vledder.

"Of course, it's possible," said DeKok. "Everything is possible. Allegedly Ella Rosseling had a motive and the opportunity. We can presume that she was in the kitchen by herself as she added the sugar . . ." He did not complete the sentence, but with an astonishingly quick movement he took his feet off the desk, grabbed his hat and started to move away.

"Where are you going?" called Vledder, taken by surprise.

"I'm going to pay a visit to the lady who replaced Ella Rosseling."

For a moment Vledder was undecided as he saw DeKok almost run out of the detective room. Several people smiled as he passed. DeKok at speed was a comical sight.

Then Vledder picked up his notebook and hastily followed his partner.

"Your servant, ma'am," said DeKok with old-world courtesy and made a slight bow, sweeping his hat off his head as he did so. "My name is DeKok . . . with kay-oh-kay. I am accompanied by my friend and partner, Vledder. We are from the police."

"Inspectors?"

"Indeed, yes. You're home alone?"

"Yes . . ."

"Excellent, really excellent," smiled DeKok. "You see, our visit is of a confidential nature. We do not want to cause you any trouble . . . that is to say, as little as possible."

She looked confused and suspicious while Vledder and DeKok both proffered their identifications. DeKok studied her. His gaze traveled from the long, strong legs to a short, leather skirt and a tight wool sweater. The oval face was surrounded by long, blond hair. The overall impression was beautiful, he thought, a classical beauty but cool, arrogant, unreachable.

"You are, I take it, Miss Kluffert."

"Yes I am. What do you want." The tone of voice confirmed DeKok's first impression. "I have little time. You come at a very inconvenient moment. I was about to leave."

DeKok smiled sweetly.

"We just want to talk to you for a moment," he explained. "We won't take much of your time. We're involved in the investigation regarding the death of Alex Delzen and we have reasons to believe," he paid particular attention to her expression, "that you . . . knew the late Mr. Delzen."

DeKok's words seemed to shock her. There was no doubt about it, thought DeKok, it was as plain as day. She made no move to hide her emotion. She lifted the back of her hand to her mouth and bit. A theatrical, but effective way to convey fright.

"You knew he was dead?"

She nodded slowly, almost imperceptibly.

DeKok looked around.

"This," he said with some emphasis, indicating the street behind him, "is not exactly the ideal setting for our conversation, don't you agree?"

She seemed to awake from a daze.

"Oh . . . I beg your pardon," she said. The door was opened wider and she allowed the two cops to step inside. "I was a bit confused," she apologized. "You see, I didn't know that anybody knew, I mean, about Alex and me."

From the spacious foyer she led the Inspectors up the stairs to a large, rectangular bedroom. The room looked neat. There was no clothing laying about and the bed was made. Green, diffused light seeped through the venetian blinds. She pointed at an arrangement in the corner.

"Please sit down."

Vledder sat down and immediately pulled out his notebook. DeKok looked skeptically at the fragile-looking chairs and wondered if they were too small for his not inconsiderable weight. He ignored the chairs and sat down on the edge of the bed.

"How did you find out about his death?"

She did not answer but walked over to a long, floor-to-ceiling mirror in a corner and rearranged her hair. The small inspection of her mirror image seemed to have restored her self confidence. She walked back to one of the fragile chairs and sat down across from Vledder. Her movements were calm, almost methodical.

"How did you find out about his death?" repeated DeKok.

She pushed her chair back a fraction, crossed her slender, athletic legs and shook her hair loose. It was a calculated gesture, designed to entice.

"I read the report of his murder in the papers." Her voice sounded soft and sad.

DeKok nodded sympathetically.

"It must have been a shock for you."

"No," she answered, shaking her head. "it wasn't a shock. I wasn't even surprised. In a way I was prepared for it."

"Prepared?"

"I knew it already," she said seriously. "I knew it *before* I saw it in the papers."

"You knew it *before* you saw it in the papers?"

"It's difficult to explain." She smiled wanly. "You wouldn't understand."

"Just try."

"I had a date with him that day," she sighed.

"The day of his death?"

"Yes, we were going to go to the theater. It had been planned for weeks. Alex would take care of the tickets and I was to meet him on the corner of the Damrak and Dam. We always met there. Alex was never late. Never. He was always very punctual, exactly on time." She hesitated. "When he didn't show up at eight o'clock, I knew something had happened to him." She gestured vaguely. "I knew right away that it was useless . . . that I didn't have to wait any longer. Alex wouldn't come . . . never again. But I didn't leave. I waited, regardless . . . I still don't know why. I didn't leave until after ten." She looked at the Inspectors. "Next morning I read in the papers that Alex had died . . . in a dirty old police station . . . murdered." It sounded like an accusation.

DeKok ignored her tone of voice.

"When Alex didn't show up on the night in question . . . why didn't you check with his rooms, with the Cluster? Surely you could have inquired if anything had happened." He hesitated for effect. "Or . . . did your relationship with Mr. Delzen not allow for such familiarities. I mean, was the relationship less intimate than that?"

A momentary sparkle brightened her eyes.

"My relationship with Alex . . . as you call it, allowed everything." She spoke in a sharp voice with a bitter undertone. "*Everything!* You hear? Everything. Alex and I . . . we loved each other, you understand, and there were no taboos, no secrets."

DeKok rubbed the bridge of his nose with a little finger.

"Strange word that," he remarked, ". . . taboo."

"Aren't you familiar with it?" She blushed.

"Oh, yes," DeKok assured her. "I'm familiar with the word. I just noted that you used it in connection with your relationship to Mr. Delzen. That's all."

Ria Kluffert suddenly rose from her chair and stood in front of DeKok. She looked magnificent. The long legs firmly planted on the floor, her hands on her hips and an angry look in her eyes. From her impressive height she looked down at the gray sleuth.

"I've the right to lead my own life!" she yelled. "Nobody is going to tell me whom to love or not to love."

"Of course," nodded DeKok, calmly, quietly. "That is correct. If you loved Alex Delzen, than that was your right. No question about it. I'd be the last person in the world to deny you that right, or to blame you for it. I'm of the opinion that it's a good thing when young people follow the voice of their heart . . . excellent, really excellent." He paused for a moment, shrugged his shoulders. "And that's why," he gestured in her direction, "I don't understand why you didn't at once go to the Brewers Canal to find out what had happened. After all . . . he was always on time . . . and you were concerned . . . worried."

"Yes," she continued, her face distorted, "yes, I was worried."

DeKok spread his arms in a gesture of surrender.

115

"Well, then why didn't you go there?"

She looked at DeKok with wide eyes. She could feel the friendly stubbornness of the big, wide man sitting on the edge of her bed. She knew his questions would return to the same subject until she had answered them to his satisfaction. At long last she would have to capitulate, would have to answer. With a sigh she let herself sink back in her chair. She folded her hands in her lap.

"My brother . . ." Her voice was barely above a whisper. "My brother didn't like Alex, didn't want me to see Alex." She bit her lower lip. "He hated him."

"Hated him . . . why?"

A sad smile played around her lips. The long, slender hands worried with the ends of her hair.

"Because of me, I think. Because of Alex's interest in me. I think . . . I think he was afraid that my . . . purity would be sullied." It sounded caustic, almost sardonic. "My purity . . ." she grinned crookedly. "The fool . . . what does he know about it." She bowed her head and her shoulders shook.

DeKok let her be. He thought she was crying, but when she looked up after a while, her eyes were dry.

"You didn't go to the Cluster that night, because you were afraid of meeting your brother." He hesitated. "Was that the reason?"

"I didn't want my brother to know that I dated Alex. He had told me several times that it had to be 'over'. Alex was bad, he said, was no good, had adventures with all sorts of women, with prostitutes. I had to end the relationship. If he ever found out that I was still seeing Alex, he would . . ." Abruptly she remained silent.

"Threats?"

"Yes," she panted, "threats." She wiped her mouth with the back of her hand and smeared some lipstick on her cheek.

116

DeKok rose with some difficulty and started to pace up and down the room. His face was serious, Something bothered him. In his mind he went over the entire visit, from the moment he had greeted her at the door. Thoughts flashed through his mind, shreds of sentences, words, reactions, expressions, hesitations, intonations . . . they all passed in review. The entire visit seemed to flash by at incredible speed, like a tape recorder at fast forward. DeKok had an uncanny gift for such mental gymnastics.

He halted behind her chair and placed his hands on her wide shoulders, the shoulders of a swimmer. The soft fragrance of violets rose from her hair. From behind her he looked at the mirrored center panel of the closet across the room and found her reflection coming back to him. Again he was struck by the tightly balanced, athletic beauty of the girl.

"You are," he said soothingly, softly flattering, "a very determined girl, brave, too. You don't strike me as the sort of woman who would forsake the love of her life." He paused, gauged the effect of his words. "And Alex . . . Alex was your great love, wasn't he?"

"I loved Alex," she said simply.

DeKok took a deep breath. He was reluctant to proceed. He would hurt the young woman and wished he could avoid it. But he saw no way out.

"And yet," he said with just a hint of reproach in his voice, ". . . and yet, you abandoned him. Even when your intuition, your feelings, told you that something had happened to him, you did not go to the Cluster . . . did not go to find out if he needed help." He shook his head wearily. "I don't understand that. Were you *that* afraid of your brother's threats?"

"Yes."

"But what could he do to you?"

He felt her body shake under his hands. Her chest rose and fell rapidly.

"What could he do to you?" insisted DeKok.

She bit her lip, trying not to answer, but finally had to let it out.

"Not me," she gasped, "Not me. He couldn't do a thing to me."

"Not you?"

"No."

DeKok leaned forward. His mouth was close to her ear.

"Who," he whispered, "who could he harm?"

She did not answer.

DeKok squeezed her shoulders slightly. There was an unhappy look in his eyes, but a determined set to his mouth.

"Why don't you answer?" he queried insistently. "After all, you know who killed Alex Delzen."

DeKok felt her nod, but the movement of her head was undetectable.

"Who?" whispered DeKok.

She bowed her head, her shoulders shook with a suppressed sob and DeKok was overwhelmed with pity.

"Ernst . . . my brother."

13

"Are we going to arrest him?"

"Who"

"Kluffert, of course." Vledder sounded surprised.

"When?" ask DeKok.

"Now." Vledder pointed at the large clock on the wall of the detective room. "It's quarter past one. We have a good chance of lifting him from his bed."

DeKok leisurely lifted both legs on top of his desk and leaned back comfortably.

"I don't know," he said, hesitating. "To be honest, I'm a bit in a quandary about it. It all seems so vague."

Vledder was astonished and showed it.

"Vague?" he snorted. "Ernst Kluffert said straight out that he would kill Alex Delzen if the latter persisted in seeing his sister." He grimaced. "It's an old-fashioned concept, I grant you, but I expect there are brothers like that. Anyway, dear sister did *not* break off her relationship with the victim and now he's dead. What else do you want? It seems like more than mere coincidence that he died on the very day he had an appointment with the woman."

"You'd make a good prosecuting attorney," smiled DeKok. "The way you state it, it does sound rather simple and straight forward. But . . . I'm afraid there won't be a judge in the country who would accept it as evidence. Where's the proof?"

"Well, yes . . . you're right," admitted Vledder disgruntled. "We don't have any proof. As a matter of fact, now that I think about it, we don't even know for sure that Kluffert knew his sister was continuing her relationship with Delzen." He spread his arms wide and sighed. "And we'd need that for the motive."

DeKok looked at him, remembering the many times that Vledder had enthusiastically promoted some way-out theory, or precipitously insisted on a particular course of action. There was a twinkle in the old man's eyes as he looked at his partner.

"Very good," he teased, "sometimes it really seems as if you're thinking."

DeKok ducked as a ledger came sailing into his direction and slapped against the wall behind him. The phone rang at that moment and, still grinning, DeKok lifted the receiver.

"There's a young man down here," said the Desk-Sergeant at the other end of the line. "He's wounded and should go to the hospital. But he insists on talking to you first. It's about Delzen."

"Who is it?"

"Duyn."

DeKok threw the receiver down and ran out of the room. Vledder followed close behind.

* * *

"To old Willie*, quick."

DeKok cast a worried look at the student and observed the pale face.

"How's it going?"

Duyn closed his eyes.

---

* Nickname for Wilhelmina Hospital, named after former Queen Wilhelmina, who reigned from 1898 until 1948, the grandmother of the present queen, Beatrix.

120

"I'll manage." The voice was weak.

The car careened around a corner. DeKok held the young man closer and felt the blood seep through the clothes.

"Stupid," he hissed from the bottom of his heart. "Whatever possessed you to come to Warmoes Street first. You should have gone directly to the nearest hospital."

"I wanted to see you first."

"Why?"

"I know who killed Alex Delzen."

"What!?"

"Haverman," nodded Duyn, tiredly, "he . . . eh, he . . ."

"Did he do this, too?"

A cramp went through the young man's body and his mouth fell open. The pained expression disappeared and he sank slowly forward. DeKok grabbed him and held him, pushed him against the back of the seat and slapped the pale face with a free hand.

"Duyn . . . did he do this, too?"

The student did not answer, but leaned weakly against the old man.

"Did he do this, too?" DeKok tried again as the car swept through the gate of the hospital and stopped in front of the Emergency Entrance.

* * *

"I hate to make an arrest that I can't make stick, later."

"How do you mean?"

"I don't want to arrest Haverman," sighed DeKok.

"Duyn quite positively identified him as Delzen's killer," said Vledder, spreading his arms in an eloquent gesture. "That's why he came to the station first, wounded and all."

121

"Indeed," nodded DeKok. "But he didn't say anything else. He didn't say what basis he had for his accusation. And a single exclamation under stress is a poor reason to arrest someone. If Duyn had told me that Haverman was also responsible for his being wounded, I wouldn't have hesitated a moment."

"But Duyn fainted."

"Yes, that was very inconvenient." DeKok stood up and started to pace through the room. As he returned close enough to Vledder's desk to make himself heard over the noise in the room, he asked: "Have you found out how he is?"

"Yes."

"Well?" asked DeKok, halting in mid-stride.

"They operated immediately." Vledder grinned bitterly. "They know how to handle that at the old Willie. It wouldn't be the first time someone is brought in with a knife wound."

"Is he in danger?"

"He was lucky. The knife slipped on a rib, it saved his life."

"So, a real murder attempt."

"Very real. The wound was close to the heart."

"An amateur," said DeKok.

"How do you know?"

"If you want to kill somebody with a knife through the heart, you must enter from below, in order to slip in between the ribs. If you stab from above, or horizontally, the knife usually hits a rib and doesn't penetrate."

"Oh."

DeKok resumed his pacing, his face was serious and he was hardly aware of his surroundings. Somebody in the house on the Brewers Canal, a member of the Cluster, was a murderer. So far he had killed once and attempted a second killing. How many more were on his list? He stopped again near Vledder's desk.

"When can we interrogate Duyn?"

"Tomorrow . . . if there are no complications."

* * *

Rudolph Hans Duyn looked pale, his narrow chest and his shoulder were wrapped in tight bandages. The long hair was soaked with perspiration and stuck to his face. A faint smile played around the pale lips.

"That was close," he whispered.

DeKok gave him a reproachful look.

"Why didn't you go see Vledder when I asked you to?"

A painful grimace replaced the weak smile as Duyn answered.

"I would have liked to help you with your investigation," he said softly. "It seemed an unique opportunity for a future criminologist. It's not everyday that a murder happens in your immediate surroundings."

"I see," answered DeKok. "And when you realized there was no way you could work with the police, you decided to unmask Delzen's killer on your own."

"Everybody is free to serve the Law. Those were your own words."

"The solving of a murder," smiled DeKok, "isn't all that simple. It takes insight and . . . experience."

"But I'm studying criminology," argued Duyn, "I'm almost ready for graduate work."

"And what does that mean?"

"That I know something about crime."

DeKok grinned.

"The prisons are full of people who know something about crime."

"You know very well what I mean," blushed Duyn. "I went about it very scientifically. I used the motive as my starting point. It's a tried and true method. If you know the motive . . . you'll find the killer."

"And you found the motive?" DeKok sounded interested.

"First I tried to figure out who could have had the opportunity to kill Alex."

"And?"

"All the students in the Cluster."

"I see. And then you figured out who had a motive?"

"Yes."

"And you drew the conclusion that only friend Haverman had enough sound reasons to help Delzen into a better world?"

Duyn pushed himself up in bed.

"It's an ideological question . . . a difference of opinion . . . principle." He paused and took a deep breath. The movement seemed to hurt him because he winced as his chest expanded. "Delzen, Haverman and myself formed a sort of troika . . . a triad. We tried to educate the students into political awareness. Delzen was a gifted speaker and an excellent debater. In more ways than one, he was the natural leader of our little sub-group."

"And Haverman objected to that?"

"No, no, not at all." Duyn shook his head vehemently. "No, Haverman did not question Delzen's leadership."

"What did he question?"

Duyn remained motionless, it was obvious that the slightest movement caused him a lot of pain.

"How can I explain it?" he asked in a sluggish voice. "It's a bit difficult, you see. The trouble was that Delzen did not represent anything. He was not the mouthpiece for some political organization, a particular group, or even a specific point of view. Delzen was Delzen . . . an ideology in itself."

"And Haverman grieved about that?"

"Grieved . . . it sounds so melodramatic." Duyn wiped his forehead which was beaded with sweat and looked at the Inspector with a sharp look in his eyes. "Students don't grieve, not anymore. It's about time that the 'Establishment' takes that into account. Ideas are important to us. Young people still maintain the capacity to fight with heart and soul for an idea . . . an ideal . . . and if necessary they'll . . . die for it."

"Or kill for it," said DeKok flatly.

The student looked pained and it was not just from physical causes.

"Murder," he exclaimed. "It keeps coming back to that. For months we have hardly discussed anything else during our debates."

"But surely you mean murder as a phenomenon . . . a fact of life?"

"That's how it started," nodded Duyn with closed eyes. "But it soon became an obsession. I told you so during our previous meeting . . . I felt it coming, it was to be expected. After all those conversations, those discussions about murder . . . murder as a typical human compulsion . . . the deed had to follow. A real murder was unavoidable."

"And Alex Delzen became the victim."

"Wim Haverman," sighed Duyn, "is a true anarchist. He considered Delzen's non-conforming attitude as treason. He told me so more than once."

"And what did he tell Delzen?"

"When he criticized Delzen for his . . . eh, ambivalent position, Alex would laugh. He didn't take politics seriously. After love, sports, philosophy . . . politics was just another stage on which he could shine. Another means to self-aggrandizement."

DeKok rubbed the bridge of his nose with a little finger. He had heard an undertone in the words of the student that seemed to indicate hate, envy, jealousy. He paused and looked at his little finger as if he saw it for the first time. He withdrew the finger and lowered his hand.

"I don't understand," he said slowly. "Surely Haverman could have distanced himself from Delzen?"

"He could not avoid Alex," grinned Duyn. "Who could? Alex was too strong . . . too much of a personality. His influence was great and became greater as time passed."

"So, he had to die," said DeKok grimly.

"Yes."

"Because of some idea . . . some ideology?

"Treason!" Duyn's voice was hoarse.

"And that's why you poisoned him, you and the others." There was utter contempt in DeKok's voice.

Duyn shook his head, forgetting his physical pain. His eyes were wide and frightened.

"No . . . not me, not me," he yelled. The sound echoed against the bare walls of the hospital room.

DeKok leaned closer.

"Haverman?"

The student plucked at the blankets, avoiding DeKok's eyes. Finally he spoke, almost slurring the words.

"Wim . . . he was going to do it. I didn't know he was going to use poison."

"I see," said DeKok with an expressionless face, "but you went along with the murder, with this . . . strictly human behavior. You didn't object."

Duyn sank back into the pillows. He was as pale as a ghost. The small red spot on the bandage slowly grew larger and brighter. The wound had started to bleed again.

DeKok was immediately contrite and worried.

"Shall I go on?" he asked, concerned. "Would you rather I came back later?"

The student slowly shook his head.

"No, it's all right," he said. "Please ask your questions. I have to get it off my mind. I won't be able to rest easy until then."

"Who stabbed you?" asked DeKok.

"I don't know . . . I don't know who stabbed me. I was in bed and asleep. Somebody must have crept into my room. I woke because of a pain in my chest and shoulder. I automatically rubbed the sore spot and felt something wet. When I put on the light next to the bed, I saw I was covered with blood. I panicked at first, but then I got out of bed and looked at myself in a mirror. I saw I had been stabbed and knew I needed medial help. I put a bandage on it, more or less, and got dressed . . . I still don't know why I didn't call for an ambulance right-a-way . . . Suddenly I realized who I had to thank for my condition . . ."

"Haverman?"

"Yes," nodded Duyn. "You see, I was the only one who knew he had killed Alex."

14

DeKok stared into the distance, his head resting on his folded hands and his elbows leaning on the edge of the desk. There was a dissatisfied look on his face. He was tormented by the feeling that he had missed something, that something was not right, in fact, absolutely wrong. There were factors he knew nothing about.

Vledder was seated across from him and was in the process of transferring his notes to the computer. Every once in a while he would glance at his partner, wondering why DeKok hesitated, seemed unwilling to take action. As far as Vledder was considered, the case was as clear as glass. It only remained to clear up a few minor points.

"As soon as Delzen died of poison," Vledder thought out loud, "Duyn immediately knew that Haverman was guilty?"

"It must have been a shock," said DeKok thoughtfully. "I don't think that Duyn realized beforehand the consequences of murder."

"But he agreed?"

"As long as they were just *talking* about," smiled DeKok tiredly, "as long as it was a matter of abstract debate . . ." He did not complete the sentence, took a deep breath. "Talking about murder is something quite different from actually doing it. When

Delzen really died, Duyn ran scared. He felt responsible, an accessory. It was something his conscience couldn't bear."

"Was that the reason he was waiting for you, posing as a hitch-hiker?"

"I presume so."

"But why didn't he mention Haverman then?"

"It wasn't about Haverman's guilt ... but about his own guilt, his guilty conscience."

"But his guilt would never be discovered," protested Vledder, "unless Haverman was caught."

"Very good," smiled DeKok, admiration in his voice. "And that's why he wanted me to go back to Amsterdam. He knew about my reputation and he fully expected that I would solve the puzzle in short order. You see, that way Delzen's murderer would be caught without him having to betray anybody ... betray Haverman."

"It might have been his death," reflected Vledder.

"You mean the stabbing?"

"Yes," confirmed Vledder. "If Duyn had mentioned Haverman to you, he would have been arrested and locked up long since. Then he could not have attempted to kill Duyn." He looked earnestly at his older partner. "I think," he continued, "that it behooves us to arrest Haverman as soon as possible. As long as he's free, Duyn is in danger."

"You really believe Haverman will try again?"

"That seems obvious," said Vledder emphatically.

They were interrupted by the telephone. DeKok stared at the instrument and then lifted the receiver gingerly.

"There's a student down here," announced the Desk-Sergeant on the ground floor. "His name is Marle and he's asking for you. He wants to talk to you."

"All right, send him up."

DeKok replaced the receiver and told Vledder.

"Marle is downstairs. He lives in the same house, doesn't he?"

"Yes," nodded Vledder, "same floor as Kluffert."

"You interrogated him?"

"Yes," answered Vledder patiently, aware that DeKok seldom liked to read reports.

"Tell me about it."

"Nothing much to tell," shrugged Vledder. "He too, like the others, believed that Delzen died as a result of suicide. A colorless figure, as I remember. I didn't learn much from him. I'm rather curious to find out what he's doing here."

"We'll soon know," said DeKok. He stood up and threaded his way through the busy room. He waited until he saw a silhouette behind the smoked glass of the door and then pulled the door open with a sudden movement. Vledder looked on from a distance. Most of the other occupants of the room, used to DeKok's sometime eccentric behavior, hardly glanced up.

A surprised young man stood in the door opening, dressed in corduroy pants and a black sweater. The inevitable sneakers on his feet.

DeKok looked him over ... demonstratively, and with a faint, arrogant smile on his face.

"Mr. Marle?" he asked, while his eyebrows danced briefly across his forehead.

The young man seemed both intimidated and intrigued.

"Hendrik Jan Marle." he announced timidly.

The gray sleuth made an inviting gesture.

"Please come in. My name is DeKok ... with kay-oh-kay. My colleague Vledder, there, across the room ... you already know him?"

"Yes, we've met."

"Excellent," declared DeKok boisterously, "really excellent." He walked a few paces into the room, grabbed a chair and

131

placed it in the middle of the room, away from the other desks. "Please sit down," he gestured. "You're here to tell us the truth this time?"

The young man seemed nonplussed and took the chair with an apprehensive look in his eyes.

"Yes . . . yes," he stammered, "that is to say . . . eh . . ."

DeKok suddenly showed anger. His friendly, craggy face became an angry mask. Only Vledder and a few of the older men in the room knew that DeKok was engaged in what Vledder was pleased to call 'theatricals'. These theatricals were a constant source of wonder and irritation to young Vledder. He always thought them to be so transparent and forced that he could not understand why people fell for it. But they did, time and time again. He edged closer and observed DeKok's "anger". Surely he thought, this time somebody will say something, will call DeKok's bluff. The student was too intelligent to be fooled by DeKok's theatricals. But the student *was* fooled, as Vledder quickly realized.

"That is to say, that is to say," mimicked DeKok. Then he raised his voice. "you have to say only one thing," he roared, "and that's the truth, nothing but the truth."

One of the suspects in a far corner of the room suddenly leaned closer to the arresting officer and started to talk, quickly and at length. Apparently he would rather confess now, than to be turned over to the wild man in the center of the room. Marle was visibly upset. He looked fearfully at a fuming DeKok.

"Yes, yes," he stuttered, completely overwhelmed. "Of course . . . the truth. I mean . . . I wanted to say that I didn't lie when I talked to your colleague . . . earlier, before, that is."

"Concealing the truth is also a lie." DeKok smiled grimly. He stamped his foot on the ground as if in the throws of a temper tantrum, walked up and down in front of the student, walked around him, muttering angry words. He seemed barely able to restrain himself from physically attacking the seated man. Meanwhile he keenly observed Marle, who had crouched down in his chair, trying to make himself smaller, hoping to disappear.

Suddenly, with a tired gesture, DeKok rubbed his face with a flat hand and pulled a second chair closer. Wearily he sank down in it.

"Sorry," he apologized, "I'm really sorry. I just lost my temper for a moment and that's dumb, inexcusable. I know. I hope you won't hold it against me." He sighed deeply. "You see, it's a complicated case, very difficult ... believe me, it's complex." He paused and gave the student a winning smile. "Such things can cause one to loose sight of the proprieties."

The changed attitude, the well-meaning friendliness, the handsome apology achieved the desired effect. The young man seemed to cheer up a little and sat straighter in his chair. A hint of a smile appeared on his face and his attitude subtly changed to one of more self-confidence.

"I understand," he said. "It's indeed a bad case for you. Complex, as you said. Especially because of the ..." He hesitated, then plunged on. "Because of the wrong impression we must have presented from the beginning. It was misleading, almost deceitful."

DeKok showed an amused smile.

"You mean the suicide theory?"

"You must understand, Mr. DeKok, the thought of murder ... a real murder seemed so silly. Unbelievable. It was as if no one among us could, or would, accept it. Also, of course, we wanted to protect our reputation, the reputation of the house, the Cluster. That's why we decided to strongly suggest the possibility of suicide during any forthcoming confrontations with the police."

"And thereby helped the killer."

"Yes," nodded Marle shamefacedly. "I realized that later. You must understand . . . the idea of suggesting suicide was an impulse. I don't think any of us thought about it in depth. We certainly had no intention of protecting the murderer. Positively not! We, we . . . we were just a bit upset, confused. Police, detectives, searching the premises. It all seemed so . . . intrusive. We wanted to be done with it as soon as possible."

"What made you change your mind?"

"What do you mean?'

"Aren't you here to tell us what you know?" DeKok sounded surprised.

Marle moved nervously in his chair.

"After last night . . . after last night it became clear to me that something had to be done and fast. Otherwise there'll be more accidents."

"What happened last night?"

"A hysterical mob, there is no other way to describe it. It seemed as if they'd all gone crazy."

"Who?"

"We, the members of the Cluster. I, too, was confused. It was all because of Duyn. He suddenly jumped up and announced that he knew Alex's killer."

"Then what?"

"There was an uproar. Duyn looked pale as a sheet. He said that he wanted to give the killer the opportunity to turn himself in. And if the murderer didn't give himself up then he, Duyn, would go to the police to tell them who was guilty."

"What was the reaction?"

"As I said," sighed Marle, "an uproar. A few of us insisted that he name the killer at once, there and then. Duyn refused. He repeated his threat. Then he turned around and left the room. We remained behind. We talked about what Duyn had said. There was a strange, tense atmosphere. We all seemed to expect something to happen. We went to bed around midnight and that's rather unusual, early I should say. But nobody wanted to talk anymore, at least not with each other."

The student paused, chewed his lower lip. Slowly he shook his head from side to side in a rhythmic, subconscious movement.

"Go on," urged DeKok.

"I couldn't sleep, I tossed and turned. Everything that had happened in the house during the last few days went through my mind. I wondered if Duyn really knew who had killed Alex. How had he gained the knowledge? And then, suddenly, I realized that Duyn was in danger. If Duyn had spoken the truth . . . if he really knew who had killed Alex . . ."

Marle paused again, closed his eyes and wiped the sweat from his forehead. This time DeKok did not urge him on. He and Vledder and a nearby detective, who did not seem to be doing anything else, waited patiently.

"I went up the stairs," resumed Marle after a long interval. "To the attic . . . to the attic room, to Duyn's room, the door was open and the light was on. But Duyn wasn't there. His bed had been slept in and there was blood on the pillow and on the sheets. I called out . . . I yelled . . . *Duyn, Duyn, where are you, Duyn?* I woke up everybody. Suddenly I stubbed my toe on something hard, something on the floor."

Marle stood up and took something out of his pocket. It was wrapped in a paper towel. He stretched out his hand to DeKok and gave him the package. Slowly DeKok unrolled the wrapping and looked at a knife, a small, sharp knife. There was blood on the blade. Marle pointed at it with a shaking finger.

"It . . . it belongs to Kluffert."

15

DeKok reacted hardly at all. He pushed his lower lip forward and looked at the knife. He brought the knife closer to his eyes and looked at the handle. He could clearly see fingerprints in the coagulated blood. Without a word, he stood up and walked over to his desk, motioning Marle to follow him. He placed the knife on his desk, pointed at a chair in front of his desk, waited until Marle sat down on it and then walked around the desk to sit down himself. Vledder had followed and now seated himself at his own desk, next to that of DeKok.

"I'm afraid," confessed Marle softly, "that those are my fingerprints. I wasn't too careful. I just picked up the knife without thinking about it."

"Who was there when you picked it up?" asked DeKok.

"Nobody . . . nobody saw I had it. I hid it in the sleeve of my pajamas."

"Why?"

"I don't know." Marle shrugged his shoulders. "I just had the feeling that nobody should see it."

"Was everybody there? I mean, when you called out, did all the students come upstairs, into the attic?"

"Yes," answered Marle thoughtfully. "Yes, they were all there . . . except Duyn. He had disappeared. I assume that he left the house under his own steam. You see, his clothes were also gone."

"He's in the hospital with a stab wound," said DeKok.

"Serious?"

"He was lucky. If everything develops the way it should, he'll be able to leave the hospital in a few days."

"May I visit him?"

DeKok shook his head.

"I've left instructions that nobody is to come near him. He's under guard, night and day. You understand, we don't want to run the risk that . . ."

"You've talked to him?"

"Yes."

"And . . . who did it?"

"That," lied DeKok, "we want to keep secret for a while." He smiled at the student. "But please, relax, I want to talk to *you* for a while. After all, you're partially responsible for what happened."

"Me?"

"Yes, you," assured DeKok. "Happily we didn't take your suggested suicide theory serious . . ." He looked from the student to Vledder, who had the grace to blush. "If we had," continued DeKok, "it could have seriously hampered our investigations. Who actually came up with the idea?"

"To suggest suicide?"

"Yes."

Marle seemed to think hard. A deep wrinkle creased his forehead and he supported his head with one hand. Vledder was reminded of Rodin's "Thinker".

"Shepherd," said Marle after a long pause. "Yes, Shepherd. It was him. He first made the suggestion." He paused again, stared at the tips of his shoes. "But," he added slowly, "I think we all immediately agreed. Especially since the suggestion came from him."

"How's that?"

"Delzen and Shepherd," smiled Marle, ". . . it's almost a concept for us. Something like Laurel and Hardy, Sears and Roebuck, Hope and Crosby. When Shepherd made the suggestion, it was as if he spoke in Delzen's name, you see, that's how close they were connected in our minds . . . they formed a unit."

DeKok thought that over. He thought about the words of the young student and tried to form an image in his own mind regarding the interconnections, the relationships within the student house.

"Laurel and Hardy," he said slowly, "Hope and Crosby . . . didn't they make the 'Road' pictures? You name comical duo's. Was there something humorous about the relationship between Shepherd and Delzen . . . something comical?"

Marle grinned.

"Delzen was by far the more dominant personality. He was Shepherd's superior in more ways than one and Shepherd freely admitted that. And it was funny, for us, to see how Delzen treated Shepherd . . . often condescending . . . I would almost say insulting, no, denigrating. But always funny, very witty." He made a sad gesture. "But Shepherd took it. He admired Delzen . . . never wanted to hear a bad word about him."

DeKok nodded his understanding.

"From what I hear," he said carefully, "the subject of murder was a frequent item of debate, especially lately. Perhaps it's just coincidence . . . but in the light of Delzen's murder a bit remarkable. Who usually introduced the subject 'murder' during those debates?"

"That's hard to say. Suddenly you're in the middle of a debate and afterward it's hard to remember who first mentioned what."

"But," observed DeKok, scratching the back of his neck, "There was little unanimity on the subject of murder, wasn't there? I heard tell that the debates could be quite heated ... intense, almost violent. Apparently opinions differed greatly."

"Yes, indeed."

"What were the main differences of opinion?"

Marle stared at the ceiling as if trying to find the answers there.

"Kluffert," he said after a while. "Kluffert and Delzen were the most diametrically opposed."

"In what way?"

"Delzen defended an opinion he called *the Right to Suicide*."

"The *right* to suicide?"

"Yes, that's what Delzen called it. According to him, a person had only one real possession and that was life. He received it at birth and lost it at the time of death. No matter what other earthly possessions a person gathered, only life itself could be termed his, or her, property. A person therefore owned this life outright, completely sovereign, and was able to dispose of it in any way he felt like."

"Including destruction," concluded DeKok.

"Exactly," agreed Marle, *"The Right to Suicide."*

"You're sure we're not talking about euthanasia, as is currently allowed. I mean, if a person is in unbearable pain, or incurable, and asks a doctor to end his, or her, life?"

"No, no. That was a different subject altogether. Delzen was talking about suicide, at any time, even at a whim."

DeKok smiled.

"Surely," he asked, sweetly sarcastic, "You don't want to suggest another suicide theory?"

Marle was visibly offended.

"Of course not," he answered emphatically. "I don't believe Delzen committed suicide. I merely tried to give you an idea of the various opinions because I thought you were interested."

DeKok made an apologetic gesture.

"I *am* interested," he said, "please continue."

"Look," said Marle, shifting in his chair, "the dispute about suicide was a direct result of the debates about suicide. You must understand that Delzen, who considered 'life' as each person's inalienable property, also opposed capital punishment. He was a violent opponent of capital punishment and called it 'legalized murder'. He was consistent in that. He considered the killing of a fellow human being as murder, no matter what the circumstances, no matter what the motive and therefore . . . anathema."

"That *does* sound rather nice, don't you think?"

"Sure." Marle nodded enthusiastically. "It *does* sound nice and as a future physician I agreed with him completely."

"Who didn't?"

"Kluffert, for one. As I said, because of his religious convictions and, of course, Haverman."

"Haverman?" asked DeKok. Vledder suddenly seemed more alert and DeKok's eyes opened wider.

Marle nodded.

"Haverman held that there were circumstances under which murder was entirely acceptable."

DeKok grimaced as if something smelled bad.

"Murder . . . acceptable?"

"Well, Haverman studies Law, you see," explained Marle. "He offered the concept of self-defence."

DeKok smiled, relieved.

"Necessary defence," he cited, "of one's own, or another's life, chastity or property."

"That's exactly what he said. He offered the classic example of two shipwrecked people in the middle of the ocean on a small raft. The raft is too small to support both. Therefore, one of the survivors must let go of the raft and drown. The question is . . . who?"

DeKok grinned.

"And thus, if one of them, pushes the other away . . . it's actually self-defence because he's preserving his own life and therefore not punishable by law. The deed has become acceptable."

"That was Haverman's argument, yes."

"I know the example," laughed DeKok, "but I have a suspicion that Haverman is a bad student. It's not an example of self–defence, but of *force-majeure*."

Marle joined in the laughter.

"No doubt you're right. There seems little difference to me between self-defence and *force-majeure*. Law doesn't interest me."

"I understand," said DeKok. "There's little of interest for a future physician. By the way . . . how did Delzen react to the example?"

"He didn't want to have a thing to do with it," declared Marle, shaking his head to emphasize the words. "Nobody had the right, no matter what the circumstance, to take the life of another . . . not even on a small raft in the middle of the ocean. In his opinion it would always be murder . . . nothing else but murder."

"What did Delzen suggest as an alternative?"

"Alex turned the argument around," laughed Marle. "He declared that one of the survivors should not allow the other to become a murderer. They should *both* leave the raft and swim until their strength gave out. According to Delzen it was better that both died, than that one would be burdened with having killed a fellow human being."

DeKok stared thoughtfully into the distance.

"That sounds very ethical."

Marle wiped his forehead.

"Yes," he agreed, "very ethical. That was Delzen. He defended his point of view in a masterly manner and, as always, with a flair all his own. But he was unable to make anybody agree with his opinion. On the whole we agreed that in that case, murder didn't enter into it and that his solution was against human nature." The student paused momentarily. "Much to Delzen's surprise, not even Shepherd agreed with him on that one."

"Was that so unusual?"

"Very much so. Shepherd *never* disagreed with Delzen's point of view." Marle grinned to himself. "Whatever Delzen wanted, was all right with Shepherd. Usually Shepherd *always* agreed with Delzen. Totally uncritical, almost child-like. But that night he gave Delzen a good argument. He even entered a new component into the debate."

"A new component?"

"It was rather difficult, as I recall." Marle wrinkled his forehead. "It was almost philosophical. Shepherd not only agreed that murder in certain cases was acceptable, he suggested that in some cases it was unavoidable. If, so argued Shepherd, someone was so threatened by another that it became a matter of life or death, him or me, in that case he felt that murder was a necessity, a compulsive requirement . . . even if murder was not in accordance with the conscience, the sensibilities, of the perpetrator. According to Shepherd, a killer could suffer from the moral burden of his deed, but still find the deed intellectually acceptable. As a clear example he mentioned *Crime and*

Punishment by Dostoyevsky, wherein an intelligent, soft-hearted student kills an old loan-shark."

DeKok rubbed the corners of his eyes in a tired gesture.

"Murder," he said languidly, ". . . the subject is nearly inexhaustible, unlike people. Anyway," he said a bit more briskly, "I must compliment you. You have an excellent memory. What was your personal point of view?"

"Regarding murder?"

"Yes."

"Life is precious," sighed Marle, "Nobody has the right to terminate it at will, not even one's own life. Otherwise I generally agreed with Delzen."

"If you feel that way," interrupted Vledder, "how are you going to react when you *are* a physician and one of your patients requests euthanasia?"

"I'll have to cross that bridge when the time comes . . . but, although it's legal, no physician is *required* to provide euthanasia. At least, not yet."

For a long time they sat silently together: the young student, a tired DeKok and a busy Vledder. Vledder was correlating the new information into his computer. Over the constant background noise of the busy room, they could hear car horns outside, an occasional raucous scream from a prostitute, the sound of breaking glass as a bottle was shattered against the pavement and shreds of a song, sung by a bunch of drunks. From the sounds DeKok determined subconsciously that it was a quiet night in the Quarter.

"Alex Delzen . . ." said DeKok, pondering. "A striking, almost pervasive personality. I would have liked to have met him alive . . . perhaps I would understand more about his death." He gave the student a wan smile. "Tell me, how was *your* relationship with him?"

Marle pursed his lips, considering.

"Friendly . . . yes, you could call it that. Sometimes he would talk to me about his worries."

"Worries?"

"Yes, Alex thought he could detect the signs of physical debility in himself."

DeKok was surprised and showed it.

"Physical debility?" he repeated, astonishment in his voice. "But Delzen was barely thirty-three years old."

"Yes," nodded Marle with a serious face, "but he was of the opinion that his vitality was not what it was supposed to be. He felt that he had lost some of his . . . eh, his virility, was less ardent than he used to be."

DeKok laughed heartily. Vledder, too, seemed amused.

"And what was the therapy prescribed by our . . . future physician?"

Marle grimaced and made a comical gesture.

"I prescribed a tonic."

"A tonic?"

"Yes."

DeKok's face suddenly changed. The amused look in his eyes had disappeared and the lines of his face flowed into an even, expressionless mask. Marle seemed not to notice the change and stared openly at DeKok. Vledder tensed.

"Did he follow your advice?" asked DeKok.

"Certainly. He bought a bottle of tonic. He showed it to me. It was a large bottle. I believe he expected miracles."

Vledder had moved behind the student. Over Marle's head DeKok looked at his assistant and saw him shake his head vigorously.

"What," asked DeKok, "happened to the bottle? It wasn't found in his room."

Marle shrugged his shoulders unconcernedly.

"The bottle has to be there," he said with simple conviction, "it wasn't nearly empty."

DeKok stared at the student with an expressionless face while his brain worked in overdrive. Suddenly, with a flash of insight, he knew what had happened to the bottle and a dread premonition came over him, seemed to paralyze him . . . but just for an instant. Then he jumped up, grabbed his hat on the run and sped toward the door.

"Hurry up," he yelled at Vledder, "before we're too late."

He was already descending the stairs when Vledder emerged from the room.

Marle remained alone, open-mouthed, in front of DeKok's desk. He was speechless, flabbergasted and looked anything but intelligent.

16

Old man Drager was dead, horribly dead.

He was found in the living room of his house on the
Brewers Canal, his head next to a cold stove and his legs next to a
turned over chair. His narrow face with the tawny skin had been
frozen in a grimace, a strange, revolting, almost demonic
grimace. The long, pointed chin jutted out and rested on the blue
swollen fingers of his left hand. A thin dribble of blood crept
from the half-open mouth and covered the gleaming yellow of a
wedding ring. Old Drager was dead, horribly dead, and DeKok
shivered visibly. He had seen more corpses than he cared to
count during his long career with Homicide, but none of them
had looked this repulsive, this loathsome.

Supporting himself by placing his hands on his knees,
DeKok rose slowly from his crouching position. His glance went
through the room. Sharply, automatically, with photographic
accuracy he identified what he saw. Every detail, no matter how
small, received the same careful scrutiny. He searched for what
he expected to find in the house of the old man, because his
fearful premonition had become such dreadful truth. It had to be
there and he found it. On a small table against the wall, almost
underneath the binoculars on their greasy strap was the bottle . . .
the large bottle of tonic that had disappeared so mysteriously

from Delzen's room. DeKok looked at it for a long time, without moving a muscle and with a hypnotized look in his eyes. It was as if the bottle mesmerized him.

Vledder stood behind DeKok. His nostrils quivered and sweat beaded his forehead. He had followed his old mentor, had watched as DeKok jumped behind the wheel of the car and he had barely been able to climb in on the passenger side when DeKok forced the car into gear. He had sat there with white knuckles as DeKok had raced through the streets and along the canals with total disregard for the vehicle, the traffic or Vledder's peace of mind. Vledder could have done it more smoothly, but probably not faster. He lacked DeKok's total knowledge of, and instinct for, every possible shortcut. All the while he had wondered where they were headed.

Until he had seen the corpse . . . the dreadful corpse and the bottle . . . half filled with tonic, a deadly tonic, mixed with parathion.

"Poisoned," panted Vledder. "Old Drager has been poisoned."

DeKok nodded slowly. He seemed to recover from his apparent daze.

"He too," sighed DeKok. "He, too, poor factotum . . . the second victim of a vile killer." He turned around and looked pensively at the distorted body on the floor. "You know, Dick," he said softly, "people like us, in our profession, we should be blessed with exceptional insight, with a particular intelligence. And not just to *solve* crimes, but to enable us to *prevent* tragedies such as this. Unfortunately it isn't the first time I came too late and I'm very much afraid it won't be the last time, either."

Vledder, ever loyal, looked at him with surprise.

"But surely you couldn't know this was going to happen, or could you?"

148

DeKok looked up, his eyes flashed. He had never lost the ability to become angry when confronted with violent death.

"I knew as much as you did," he said sharply. "I knew that you had not found the poison that killed Alex Delzen. I thought it strange and I wondered about what could have happened to it. But I was more concerned with *how* Delzen could have ingested the poison." He grinned mockingly. "A murderer can hardly invite his intended victim to swallow poison. Therefore it must have happened in another way, it had to be sneaked into him, he had to be tricked."

He paused, shook his head ruefully.

"That Delzen worried about his potency, his physical debility and that he used a tonic for that, you see, Dick, that . . . that I know now," he glanced at his watch, "for exactly fifteen minutes." He bit his lower lip. "Too late to save this old man."

Vledder bowed his head. DeKok's biting, almost cynical tone of voice touched him, but did not hurt. He was ashamed for another reason. He deplored his own ineptness, his lack of insight, his inexperience, all of which combined to make it difficult at times to follow the thought processes of his older partner. It happened still far too often that he did not understand DeKok and he groped hesitatingly, fumbling for his true intentions. It irritated him . . . it irritated him much more than the sarcastic hints DeKok dropped from time to time. He knew the gray sleuth used that tone to help stimulate his ideas, to force Vledder to think.

"But," he asked diffidently, "how did you know you would find the bottle here?"

"I didn't know," denied DeKok. "I just had a feeling, a terrible suspicion and I hoped, against hope, that the old man hadn't tried any of it. That's why I went a bit crazy in the car. But the feeling that old Drager had the bottle, wasn't all that surprising. It was to be expected."

149

"To be expected?"

"Old man Drager, God rest his soul, was a voyeur, a Peeping Tom, who enjoyed Delzen's amorous adventures from a distance, from the privacy of his own room. As we know, Delzen trusted Drager to a certain extent. He exchanged small confidences with him. Therefore it's safe to assume he had told him about the tonic and just possibly somewhat exaggerated the stimulating effects. Didn't Marle say . . . he expected miracles?"

"That's what he said," agreed Vledder.

DeKok raised a forefinger in the air.

"You see," he went on, "the fact that Drager took Ella Rosseling's slip from Delzen's room, made me think. It seemed so senseless. What use was a black lace slip to an old man. What could he do with it? Nothing, at first glance. Unless . . . unless it was a matter of identification."

"Identification?" Vledder was puzzled.

"Yes. Drager, I realized, basked in the reflected glory of Delzen's conquests. It was an example for him, an example he could not hope to follow because the old man, naturally, no longer was as virile as a man in the bloom of his life, a man like Delzen." DeKok raked his fingers through his hair. "Perhaps you remember that I asked him if he had taken anything else from the room, in addition to the slip. He denied it, but I had the feeling he lied. Not until Marle mentioned the tonic, did I realize that Drager had taken it."

Vledder swallowed.

"The tonic," he said tonelessly, "the tonic with parathion."

DeKok nodded. He picked up the bottle with the tips of his fingers on the neck and held it up to the light. He read the label.

"Stimulating," he read, "Arousing, restores vigor and vitality."

They looked at the corpse. Its contorted grimace stared back at them.

150

A simple phone call alerted the *Thundering Herd* and within half an hour the place was crawling with photographers, fingerprint experts, forensic specialists, a Chief Inspector, a representative from the Judge-Advocate's office and there was even somebody from the Department of the Interior, the Home Secretary's office, under which the Dutch police ultimately resorts. Bram Weelen, DeKok's favorite photographer was there and so was old Ben Kruger, the dactyloscopist.

Only the Coroner was missing, but he had sent two of his attendants and had promised to meet Dr. Rusteloos, the police surgeon who was to do the autopsy, at the police lab.

DeKok kept out of the way, smiled at the crowd and listened with feigned attention to some of the silly suggestions with which he was bombarded. With the exception of Weelen, Kruger and a few forensic people, DeKok had little use for the bunch of smug, self–important experts and official curiosity seekers.

When, in DeKok's opinion, it had lasted long enough, he nodded to the two men from the Coroner's office. Without ceremony they pushed through the crowd of officials and belted the corpse to the stretcher. The way in which they manoeuvred the corpse down the narrow staircase showed a lot of experience and unemotional professionalism. DeKok caught Vledder's eye and they left without being noticed.

Outside DeKok sucked his lungs full of fresh air. He was glad to be back in the street. The atmosphere in the little room had been suffocating. He crossed the road to the water's edge and stopped. With his hands in his pockets, a frown on his face and his little hat pushed far back on his head, he stared across the murky water toward the other side of the canal. He saw vague silhouettes behind the windows of *Disputa Hora Ruit.*

"Time passes," remarked Vledder, reading his mind.

"Yes," agreed DeKok. "Let's go tell the members of the Cluster that they'll have to advertise for a new factotum."

17

Student Gelder shook his head in sad commiseration.

"Poor Mr. Drager," he said, ". . . dead. Terrible. He was such a friendly and considerate old man. It's hard to believe. When did he pass away?"

"Last night, I think. When did you see him last?"

"Yesterday morning, yes, around ten o'clock. I met him downstairs in the corridor and he asked if I needed anything. He also used to get the groceries, you know . . . and if we wanted something special . . ." The student sighed. "How did he die?"

"By poisoning."

"Poisoning?" Gelder was surprised.

"Parathion," grimaced DeKok, "an insecticide."

"Just like Delzen."

DeKok nodded slowly and looked intently at the student.

"And not voluntarily . . . not as a grotesque demonstration against pollution, but because . . . he thought he could find back a piece of his youth."

Gelder blushed.

"Not a heroic suicide, you mean." He smiled shyly. "I understand you and your colleague won't believe *that*."

DeKok sat down on the edge of the bed in the roomy bed-sitter and placed his hat on the bed next to him.

"Where's friend Haverman?"

"I don't know."

"We were in his room next door." DeKok gestured. "It seems that the bed has not been slept in."

Gelder sank down in an old rattan chair. DeKok wondered idly what students would use to furnish their rooms if there were no rattan furniture. Student housing in the city was at a premium. Dutch universities do not provide dormitories. Students rent rooms with families, or as in this case, rented, or bought a house which was then subdivided. But in almost all student rooms, he had found, the furniture consisted of a bed, a desk, bookshelves and rattan furniture, lots of rattan furniture.

"That's right," said Gelder, interrupting DeKok's thoughts. "Wim Haverman has gone away. I haven't seen him since the incident with Duyn."

"Escaped?"

The student took off his glasses and breathed on them.

"What do you expect me to say to that?"

DeKok jumped up, eyes flashing. His face became a mask of wrath.

"The truth . . . that's all . . . we have no time to waste and I'm not about to listen to any more fairy tales." He took the student by the front of his shirt and shook him. "Again . . . *where's Haverman!*"

Johan Gelder paled. He had not expected this sudden rage from the mild-looking, friendly old man. The strength in DeKok's arms astonished and frightened him.

"I . . . I d-don't know," Gelder managed to say in a shaking voice. "Believe me, I don't know where he is. I never saw him leave. I swear, that's all I know. But he *did* seem upset."

"What do you mean?"

"He . . . he, eh, he looked a bit strange, I thought, confused. He mumbled something about everything being wrong . . . a mistake. And that I should say goodbye to the others."

"Then what?"

"Then he left."

DeKok released the student. He walked over to the wall and looked at the reproduction of a Renoir. After a while he turned around.

"Parathion," he said slowly, "is an insecticide. A very fast–acting and deadly poison. You know that, Mr. Gelder. As a future biologist you are aware of the destructive effect upon the organism. You also know how simple the poison is to obtain . . . and to administer." He moved away from the wall, slowly, listlessly. He stopped in front of the student, legs spread, in a threatening attitude. "Mr. Gelder, did you have reasons to want Alex Delzen dead?"

The student looked at him, his lips aquiver.

"And did you think that I would use parathion?"

DeKok reacted sharply. He leaned forward and brought his face to within inches of that of the student.

"That is not an answer to my question," he hissed, "You better . . ." He stopped abruptly and his eyes turned away. He had heard a sound in the room next door, the vague, furtive sound of shuffling footsteps. He brought his lips close to Gelder's ear and pointed. "Haverman's room?" he whispered.

Gelder nodded.

"Somebody's there," breathed the student tensely.

DeKok slowly rose from his leaning position and stepped out of the room. Vledder followed close behind. On their toes they slinked down the corridor and stopped in front of Haverman's room. Carefully DeKok turned the knob. He hesitated for a moment, then pushed open the door with a sudden movement.

A young woman stood in the middle of the room, a suitcase in her hand. A ray of sunshine played with her chestnut brown hair. She looked with amazement at the two men in the door opening, as if the view paralyzed her. Slowly the suitcase slipped from her fingers and fell to the floor with a thud.

The gray sleuth smiled.

"My name is DeKok," he introduced himself.

" . . . with kay-oh-kay," completed Vledder with a mocking twinkle in his eyes.

* * *

DeKok approached her, admiring her slender, almost boyish figure. He stopped in front of her and with an expression of friendly attention, he asked his first question.

"Who are you?"

She pulled back her head slightly, like an animal that has been approached too close and shook her long hair. She had recovered from the initial shock. She took a step back and the look in her eyes was cool, challenging.

My name is Louise . . . Louise Kamerik," she said with spirit, "Lou to my friends."

"You live here?" smiled DeKok.

"No."

The gray sleuth feigned amazement.

"In that case, can you explain your presence in this room?"

She cocked her head at him, the lustrous hair falling to one side.

"I could," she said slowly, "I could . . . but I don't intend to tell you."

Vledder held his breath. DeKok's eyebrows rippled briefly, too fast for the human eye to follow.

156

"That doesn't seem very smart," he commented mildly. "If you will not give me a reasonable explanation, I will have to interpret the situation as I see it. You see, I'll have to provide my own explanation."

She shrugged her shoulders.

"Go ahead, do what you must." She sounded nonchalant, as if she did not care.

DeKok pursed his lips. Carefully he took her by an arm. There was a sad look in his eyes.

"Louise Kamerik," he spoke formally, "you're under arrest for breaking and entering and . . . *casu quo* attempted theft."

She looked up at him, her mouth fell open in surprise.

"You can't mean that!"

DeKok nodded with a melancholy face.

"I mean it," he said dejectedly. "You leave me no other choice. How else can I explain your presence here?"

She pulled her arm away, lost some of her self-control.

"I'm no thief . . . and you know it."

DeKok sighed.

"I know," he said patiently, "that you entered this room with an empty suitcase and, without our intervention, would have left again."

"With the same suitcase," grinned Vledder, "but full of loot."

For a moment she was undecided. She glanced from DeKok to Vledder and back again.

"All right," she said resignedly, "you win. I came to get some clothes and things for Wim."

"He sent you?"

"Yes."

DeKok looked at her.

"Then you know where he is," he stated.

She pressed a row of small, sparkling white teeth into her lower lip.

"Wim didn't do it."

"What!?"

"He didn't poison Alex Delzen . . . and he also didn't stab anybody." She shook her head with vigor. "Wim wouldn't do anything like that."

"Then . . . why is he in hiding?"

"Ruud is crazy." She swallowed.

"Ruud? Rudolph . . . Rudolph Duyn?"

"You mustn't believe him."

"What shouldn't I believe," asked DeKok sharply, "the stab wound in his chest?"

She stamped her foot on the floor. Suddenly she resembled a small child with a temper tantrum.

"He didn't do it," she cried, "I told you, Wim wouldn't do a thing like that."

"He had every possible motive," barked DeKok. "And time was running out. Duyn had announced he would inform the police."

She suddenly clapped her hands to her face and began to cry in earnest.

"It's all wrong," she sobbed. "It's a mistake."

DeKok seemed without pity.

"When Haverman realized," he continued heartlessly, "That his attempt had failed and that Duyn was still alive, he panicked and took flight."

Louise Kamerik looked at him with a teary face, but she suddenly seemed calm, strangely and unnaturally calm.

"Wim has told me you would think that way." Her deep voice sounded hoarse. She nodded to herself. "That's the way cops think. Perhaps it's meant to be that way . . . maybe it's a good thing . . . perhaps a cop can't think any other way." Again she looked at DeKok. "But it isn't true!" Furiously, she suddenly attacked him. Her tiny fists drummed on his broad chest. "It isn't true!" she screamed.

DeKok let her be. When she had recovered from her rage, he led her calmly, but decisively to an easy chair, a rattan easy chair, and forced her to sit down. He sat down across from her on the edge of the bed.

"I don't understand your anger," he said softly, in a friendly tone of voice. "The police think the way Haverman expects them to think. Isn't that just perfect? And now you tell me it's wrong, a mistake. Well, I'm open to suggestions."

She rubbed her eyes with a lace handkerchief, blew her nose and wiped the hair out of her eyes.

"Wim is so impractical, a scatterbrain," she said calmly. A tired smile played around her lips. "Maybe that's why I love him so much. He's so honest . . . so impassioned . . . so full of ideals. He would be ready to plow the whole earth with his bare hands if he thought it could change the world, make it better."

"Different from Delzen," understood DeKok.

A shadow fled across her pixie face.

"Delzen was Delzen . . . solely for the sake of Delzen."

"A concise analysis," admired DeKok.

Her cheeks regained some color.

"Alex had no real ideals, no grandiose ideas. He wasn't inspired, not fanatic enough."

"And that's a requirement, is it?"

"Of course it is." Her eyes flashed. "Of course that's a requirement. *Real* ideals leave no room for concessions. You have to be able to sacrifice anything for them. Everything else has to take second place."

"Including love?"

She hesitated, the corners of her mouth quivered nervously.

"Including love," she said softly.

DeKok rubbed the bridge of his nose with a little finger. Then he looked at it pensively for a while, as if wondering what to do with it next. He lowered his hand and asked the next question.

"How well did you know Alex Delzen?"

"What do you mean by that?" she asked, suspicion in her voice.

"Just what I asked," answered DeKok, making a nonchalant gesture. "How well did you know Alex Delzen?"

Louise Kamerik lowered her eyes. Her small fingers worried the hem of her skirt.

"Very well," she whispered, "very well. Alex was a friend."

"And you broke off the relationship in favor of Haverman?"

"Yes."

"And that was the end of it?"

She shook her head slowly.

"Alex kept pursuing me . . . waited for me after classes . . . wrote letters. Alex . . . Alex couldn't stand to lose."

"And Haverman knew about it?"

"Knew what?"

"That Delzen still persisted in seeing, pursuing you?"

She looked DeKok full in the face. Suddenly all color had drained from her face. Her light-brown eyes were filled with fear. In despair she shook her head.

"No," she uttered breathlessly, "no, it isn't that. You're thinking all wrong again. You don't understand . . . you just don't understand." Again she clapped her hands to her face and started to cry all over again. DeKok stood up and saw Vledder's reproachful looks.

"What is it?" he asked softly.

"Was that necessary?" hissed the young Inspector.

DeKok passed him and walked out into the corridor. For the second time that day he needed fresh air.

18

DeKok was sprawled behind his desk in the large detective room, his legs resting on a pulled-out drawer. The old cop had tired feet. It was as if thousands of tiny, little devils were using the balls of his feet and his calves as a pincushion for as many tiny, red-hot pins. He could almost hear the gleeful, sadistic shouts of the tiny red devils. The pain crept up from his feet, engulfed his shins and seemed to throb in the hollow of his knees. A paralyzing, incapacitating feeling. It was a bad sign.

When a case was at a dead end, when he was on the wrong track, when he seemed to move farther and farther from a solution, the little devils went to work. When things went right, when he was making progress, he could walk for hours, days, weeks and never give his feet and his legs a second thought. But when things went wrong, then . . .

He looked up at Vledder, standing next to his desk.

"You weren't too happy, this afternoon?"

The young Inspector shrugged his shoulders.

"The girl made a favorable impression on me. Sweet, soft, a bit helpless. I thought you were too hard on her."

"I thought so too," nodded DeKok. "But two corpses and an attempted murder leave little room for sentiment. Did you make any appointments?"

"She's coming here, tonight at ten and she'll bring Haverman."

"So . . . good work."

"She promised me faithfully . . . but on one condition."

"What's that?"

"That you won't arrest him."

"What did you say to that?"

"That we never arrest *innocent* people," smiled Vledder.

"Excellent, really excellent. A diplomatic answer."

"Do you think Haverman is guilty?"

"I don't know." DeKok sounded irked.

"But he took off."

"It could have been fear," excused DeKok. He lifted his tired feet off the drawer and gently lowered them to the floor. He closed the drawer and pushed his chair back. "We can safely assume," he continued, "that both Duyn and Haverman must, from time to time, have toyed with the idea of getting rid of Delzen. They were always talking about murder and there's no smoke without fire. I mean, if they were talking about it, they must have been thinking about it. Then, when Delzen *was* killed, Duyn decided that it had to be Haverman. It seemed obvious to him. But . . . imagine yourself in Haverman's shoes if he was *not* guilty."

"Uncomfortable, to say the least," agreed Vledder. "Especially after Duyn's announcement that he would inform the police."

"Exactly. Duyn manoeuvred Haverman into a corner from which there was no escape. Whether innocent or guilty . . . it made no difference. That's why he took off and that's why we should not necessarily see his flight to his girl-friend as detrimental to his case. He might just have been afraid."

"Afraid of us?"

"Yes, afraid of being arrested."

"You now want to eliminate him as a suspect?"

"Most assuredly not." DeKok shook his head vigorously. "Haverman *could* be the person who poisoned Delzen. He's almost an ideal suspect. Especially if we forget all about ideologies, politics and the like, but look at it in the light of competition for Louise."

"It's almost certain he stabbed Duyn," sighed Vledder.

"Why?"

"The announcement Duyn made was meant to alert Haverman, warn him. Therefore Haverman was interested in making sure that Duyn would forever hold his peace."

DeKok considered that.

"Unless," he said after a short interval, "someone else felt threatened by Duyn's announcement."

They remained silent, each wrapped up in his own thoughts. After a long pause, Vledder spoke again.

"I would like to return to Drager's death, for just a moment," he said pensively. "There are a few things that bother me, that don't compute."

"Such as?"

"If I understood you correctly, earlier, the killer had not meant to kill the old man. I mean, it wasn't so much murder, as an accident. Death by misadventure."

DeKok nodded.

"You could call it that," he said, "but legally you should probably call it 'involuntary manslaughter'. In Holland we call that 'death by guilt', an old-fashioned term, but it holds the killer responsible. The murderer had no way of knowing that Drager would take away the bottle, he could not have foreseen that. But if he had not introduced the poison into the bottle, Drager would be alive. So, he's responsible for the death. In my mind there's nothing 'involuntary' about it. It's like leaving a loaded gun laying around. When a child kills someone with it, I feel the person who left it laying around is just as guilty, maybe more so."

"Uhuh," grunted Vledder, who was familiar with DeKok's stern views on responsibility. He had heard DeKok accuse a wayward husband of driving his wife to prostitution. "If you hadn't left your wife," DeKok had argued, "she would not have been forced into prostitution to support herself and the children."

"But," resumed Vledder, irritation in his voice, "I don't understand why the murderer left the bottle in the room. Why didn't he remove the bottle as soon as Delzen had left the house? He ran a fearful risk, after all. That bottle, if I had found it in time, would have pointed a finger at the killer. Apart from the fact that he ran the risk of killing additional, innocent victims. Like Drager, for instance."

DeKok raked his fingers through his hair.

"Old Drager was too greedy, too quick. He was just one step ahead of the murderer. Also, you must realize that the killer couldn't know that his attempt had succeeded until he heard that Delzen was dead. Because he mixed the parathion with the tonic, he could never be sure of the exact time that Delzen would drink it. He could only wait until Delzen felt like taking a swig."

Vledder nodded thoughtfully.

"Pretty cunning, when you think about it," he said with a hint of admiration. "I mean, to use the tonic as a vehicle for the poison. I bet Delzen didn't even notice it, didn't taste it. That tonic has an odd taste, anyway."

DeKok did not answer. He rubbed his legs with a long-suffering gesture. When he straightened up, he said:

"Please make sure that brother and sister Kluffert are here at ten o'clock tonight. I want to talk to them."

"Also at ten?"

"Also at ten," confirmed DeKok. He waddled over to the coat rack and started to put on his raincoat.

"Where are you going?" asked Vledder.

"I feel like a drink," smiled DeKok. Vledder knew what that meant. DeKok was going to have one, or more cognacs at his favorite bar.

* * *

Threatening cumulus clouds had come in from the West and had conquered the friendly blue sky. The sun was hiding behind a thick, gray, mass from which a ground-soaking drizzle descended on the roof tops of Amsterdam and the surrounding low lands. DeKok stood on the worn out steps of the ancient police station and stared up at the narrow strip of dirty sky that was visible from his vantage point. "Oh, land of mist and manure," he recited. It was the only sentence he remembered from a poem he had learned in his youth. He pulled the old raincoat closer around himself and tied the belt in a knot. Then he pushed his little felt hat tighter on his head and ventured out into the street.

Alex Delzen's murder bothered him for several reasons. In the first place because he despised poisoning more than any other form of killing. It was too anonymous, too impersonal, not emotional enough. Secondly he disliked the environment in which the murder had taken place. He did not necessarily dislike students, not at all. He could appreciate them . . . admired their dedication and their jokes. As long as they remained jokes. But this particular bunch of students had stopped playing. The carefree student days had disappeared, had made way for serious business . . . gray, somber, aggressive objectives. One of them had killed Alex Delzen. In cold blood, with cold, calculated premeditation. DeKok pondered the situation. Alex Delzen . . . the last buccaneer. The eternal student from a bygone age. A man who wrote life with a capital letter L. In fact there was no motive, at least it seemed that way, because one never knew with students. They did not fit within the overall scheme of things. Technically adult, but practically still children, especially after two or three years, when they thought they had all the answers. Who was it that said: "the more I know, the less I know"? he couldn't remember, but he agreed with it. Students never seemed to achieve that particular level of wisdom. What code was used to kill Delzen? What sort of twisted justice was used as an excuse? He sighed deeply. How would he ever find out?

He passed *Onse Lieve Heer op Solder* (Our Dear Lord in the Attic), the dearest museum he knew. Then he turned right and wended his way deeper into the Red Light District, crossed Old Church Square, went across a narrow bridge toward Old Acquaintance Alley and eventually sidled into the bar on the corner of Barn Alley, the establishment of his long-time friend Little Lowee.

He wiped a hand over his wet face and peered through the heavy, leather-bordered curtains into the dimly lit space. Then he parted them and walked over to the bar and hoisted himself on the stool in his usual spot at the end, his back to the wall.

Little Lowee, so called because of his stature, wiped his hands on a spotted apron and came over with a big smile on his mousey face.

"Well, well, Mr. DeKok," he said cheerfully. "I ain't half glad to see you back. How many pikes did you catch then?"

DeKok suddenly realized that he had not visited Lowee's bar since he had come back from his short fishing vacation. He had simply been too busy.

"Pour first, Lowee," he laughed, "and I'll tell you some fish stories."

The diminutive barkeeper grabbed a bottle from under the counter without looking and with the same motion placed two large snifters on the bar in front of DeKok. It was a special bottle, kept there for DeKok's exclusive use, but Lowee always had a drink with the old cop. It was a tradition that went back more than twenty-five years, since DeKok's days in uniform.

DeKok watched with pleasure as Lowee performed his magic with the bottle. DeKok enjoyed moments like this. Cognac was more than a drink to him, it was almost a devotion. The ceremony was as important as the taste. He listened to the gurgling sound as the liquid filled the glasses and he anticipated the heavenly aroma and that first, blissful sip.

They lifted their glasses, the cop and the barkeeper who had probably broken all of God's commandments at one time or another and broken most of man's laws with it.

"To crime," they said simultaneously.

After the first glass, DeKok told Lowee about the pikes he had not caught. Lowee laughed heartily.

"And they say them fishes is stupid," he said. He slapped the top of the bar with pure joy. "Nossir, I thinks they's smarter than people. Iffen you cain't catch 'em, they's smarter than wise guys."

DeKok laughed and enjoyed his cognac. In retrospect, he thought, life was not so bad. One had to lighten up a little, not be too serious. *That* was the trick. From somewhere he remembered a saying: *Go with the flow*. He was not sure what it meant, but it seemed to express his feelings at the moment. He had a second glass and he felt the pain in his legs slowly dissipate. It improved his mood considerably.

"Pour me another one, Lowee," he said jovially, "I've been too long without it."

Lowee obeyed with the alacrity of a good publican.

After the third glass DeKok felt the "manure and mist" withdraw to a far corner of his mind. He was ready to face the world again with a more optimistic view. He was again able to see the sun behind the clouds. But that was as far as he went. The sky was not clear blue again. The murder of Alex Delzen remained like a threatening thundercloud, shutting out the sun.

"You know Ella Rosseling?" he asked Lowee.

"A working girl?"

"I think so."

"What she look like?"

"Beautiful, of course." DeKok shrugged his shoulders. "And young. She wears black, lace slips and she visits her clients."

Lowee laughed.

"Tha's all you got?"

"I'm afraid so."

Little Lowee thought about it. It was a visible effort. His mousey face screwed up into a painful expression. Finally he spoke.

"Ask Flemish Trixy," he said. "Reckon she can help you. She keeps a lotta of them irregulars."

DeKok knew what he meant. A prostitute who had her "own" window, could always be found in the same place, was a "regular". As such she would more than likely be known to Lowee, who knew almost everybody in the Quarter. An "irregular" was a part-time prostitute, or one who made house calls. In between house calls, they might fill in for a "regular" who was on vacation, or otherwise indisposed, or they would work out of a brothel. Flemish Trixy kept a house where she rented window space to "irregulars" on a daily, or weekly basis.

DeKok thanked the small barkeeper, drained his glass and left the bar as if he was walking on clouds. The pain had completely left his legs. Outside he realized, much to his surprise, that the rain was still pouring down. It was a sobering experience.

19

The old house of Flemish Trixy near the Rear Fort Canal was a sweet little brothel with accommodations for three prostitutes, each with their own room, complete with a seating arrangement, a shower, a large mirror and a bed. Everything clean and in good repair.

Flemish Trixy was a clean person in her habits and her surroundings and the women she allowed to practice the world's oldest profession in her establishment were carefully chosen for personal and professional cleanliness. Of course, she also took care to take into consideration the more obvious female attractions. After all, Trixy operated a brothel and that was never meant to be a charitable organization.

DeKok had known her for some time, but she was one of those Madams who never came into contact with the police. Her clients, too, seemed to conform to Trixy's ideas of what was clean and proper.

She received DeKok in her private room, a large farm kitchen, which smelled of furniture polish, soap and the most aromatic coffee this side of Belgium. Flemish Trixy, as her name implied was from Flanders in Belgium and the Belgians make a fetish out of coffee. DeKok took off his dripping raincoat and wet hat and placed them on the counter in the kitchen part of the large room. Then he joined Trixy in the part that had been decorated as an old-fashioned Dutch living room, with heavy curtains, a Turkey carpet and solid, oak furniture. From this room, which was as spotless as the rest of the establishment, Trixy dispensed condoms, made change and provided an endless supply of clean towels. A blackjack was clearly visible on a side board, to be used for the occasionally unruly client. For Trixy was an independent business woman and was her own bouncer.

"I don't know if you can help me," began DeKok.

She gave him a naughty look.

"You," she said sweetly, "can always find a haven here."

"I'm looking for Ella Rosseling," said DeKok, ignoring the barely veiled enticement.

"Ella Rosseling," she nodded. "That's right, she's with me. Why? Has she done something?"

"No, I just want to talk to her."

She stood up, went to the window, pushed a curtain aside and looked into what could best be described as a large rear-view mirror. It was not an unusual arrangement for a brothel. By means of a ingenious set of mirrors, the entire facade of the building could be observed at all times.

"You'll have to wait a moment," she said, "she has a visitor."

DeKok nodded his understanding.

"Will it take long?"

Trixy laughed.

"That depends on how sweet the john is."

"You mean," corrected DeKok, grinning, "how much money he wants to spend."

"Well," she shrugged her shoulders, "isn't that the same thing?"

DeKok dropped the subject but eagerly accepted a cup of Trixy's really excellent coffee.

"Milk and sugar."

"Just sugar," answered DeKok. "It's bad weather for business," he continued, "it's raining cats and dogs."

"Ach," she said, spooning sugar in his coffee, "those in need will find my door, regardless." It sounded like an appropriate Bible text. "As you can see, all the girls are occupied."

DeKok comfortably slurped his coffee. He saw nothing incongruous about spending the time of day chatting with a brothel keeper.

"How long has she been with you?"

"Ella?"

"Yes."

"Almost a year . . . off and on."

"Where is she from?"

"The Hague, I think. Her parents live there."

"Of age?"

"She wouldn't be in my house, otherwise," grinned Trixy.

"Married?"

"No."

"How old?"

"Twenty-two . . . just."

"A pimp?"

"No pimps in my house." Flemish Trixy looked stern. "As soon as I know that the girls have a pimp, I kick them out. I want no trouble."

DeKok smiled at the vehement tone.

"You ever hear of an Alex Delzen?"

"No . . . who's that?"

"A student . . . tall, dark and handsome."

"The name doesn't mean a thing to me." She shook her head and pushed her chair closer to the table. "There used to be a student who came here."

"For Ella?"

"Yes."

"What was his name?"

"That I don't remember, the name just escapes me . . . but it wasn't Delzen."

"Did he come regularly?"

"Well . . . regularly . . . if you put it that way . . . he's been here once or twice."

"Strange that you still remember."

She grinned boyishly. The years seemed to fall away and her round, wrinkled face was almost pretty.

"Of course I remember, I had to kick him out in the street myself."

"Oh . . . why? Did he cause trouble?"

She pushed her chin forward and snorted.

"I would say so. The last time he came . . . he's no sooner inside, or he attacks Ella. Just like that . . . took her by the neck. I swear to you . . . he would have killed her if I hadn't been right there. Dammit . . . that boy was completely crazy, out of control, foaming at the mouth."

"I never heard anything about that. No police?"

"Here," smiled Trixy, "I take care of my own business. I'm not all that old and decrepit yet. I don't need no cops to upset my girls and my customers. Here, look." She raised an arm and showed him the bulge of biceps.

DeKok grinned at the display of power.

"But why did that boy act so crazy?"

"Who knows," she shrugged. "I never even bothered to ask. He was just angry with Ella. He cursed her as a whore, a slut, he called her every name in the book."

"He did . . . the student?"

"What do you think," grinned Trixy, "you think students are too refined to know bad words?"

174

It was not what DeKok had meant at all, but he nodded seriously.

"Still," he said ". . . there must have been a reason."

"Well, you better ask Ella about that, then."

* * *

"My name is DeKok . . ."

She gave him a challenging smile.

" . . . with kay-oh-kay," she completed playfully. "Oh, I've heard *stories* about you. From the girls . . . they all know you."

"A dubious honor."

"You think so?" She laughed again.

The old Inspector stood on the threshold of her room. Wide, massive. His large frame almost touched the doorposts on either side. From his height he looked down on her. She was naked and seated on the bed, her back to the wall. She had pulled up her long, slender legs and folded her arms around her knees. Temptation gleamed in her clear green eyes. It was a professional look, but not any less enticing for all that. DeKok wiped a hand across his dry lips. With some difficulty he forced an official expression on his face.

"I wanted to talk to you."

"What about?"

"Alex Delzen."

Her tone and her attitude changed at once. Angrily she jumped up, grabbed a dressing gown from a nearby chair and pulled it on, her back to him.

"Who told you about Alex and me," she asked, turning around, closing the buttons on the dressing gown. "That dirty old man?" There was suspicion in her voice.

"Who's the dirty old man?" asked DeKok.

"That's what Alex called him. You know who I mean, the old man from the Cluster . . . who took care of all the errands and such."

"I know who you mean." DeKok nodded slowly. "But it wasn't the dirty old man. He's dead. He died of the same poison that ended Alex Delzen's life."

She was visibly upset.

"Oh," she said, shaken. "I didn't know that . . . that old man . . . dead. When? Darn it . . . that's a shock. Terrible. Murdered as well?"

DeKok was pleasantly surprised by the "darn it". It sounded so old-fashioned. Not at all the sort of thing to be expected from a prostitute. He looked at her with new interest. But he did not answer her question. He had denied getting her name from old Drager. It was a deliberate lie. Ella Rosseling frowned prettily, she was thinking and came to the wrong conclusion.

"Then it must have been Mannie," she said vehemently. "He must have told you about Alex and me, I mean. He was the only other person who knew."

"Who's Mannie?"

"It's a nickname."

"For who?'

"Emanuel . . . Emanuel Shepherd, the so-called friend of Alex."

DeKok studied her face.

"So-called? You don't think Shepherd was a real friend to Alex?"

She grimaced, pushed the hair from in front of her face.

"He's a sneak."

"That sounds less than flattering."

She snorted contemptuously.

"The fool . . . he almost strangled me . . . right here in the house, he took me by the throat . . . just because I had told Alex what a pitiful character he was."

"Shepherd . . . pitiful?"

She sighed deeply, her breasts moved up and down, strained against the thin material of the dressing gown.

"It was dumb of me," she admitted, irritation in her voice. "I should have said nothing." She shook her head and pulled her gown tighter against her body. "It was just dumb . . . real dumb." She paused. "You see," she continued haltingly, "a girl like me . . . we want something of our own, once in a while, right?" She leaned forward and slapped a flat hand on the bed. "This . . . this, you see, is business. It doesn't touch you." She smiled shyly. "And, as I said, every once in a while you want something, something real. After all, I'm a healthy girl." She sighed again. "And with Alex I could be myself. He knew I was in the life, but he understood. It didn't bother him."

She stared dreamily at DeKok, but did not see him. Her memories were lost in a sweet past. After a long pause she continued.

"Alex introduced me to Shepherd. *My friend Emanuel,* he said, *we call him Mannie.* But . . ." She smiled sadly. "I saw at once that he wasn't a true friend."

"How?"

"He was too friendly . . . excessively so. Too obvious. He was dirty . . . flattering . . . slippery. You know what I mean? He wasn't *real*. He stank."

"He didn't wash?"

"No, no, dirty . . . unwholesome."

She groped on the table behind her and found a pack of cigarettes and a lighter. She lit the cigarette with shaking hands.

"And I was right," she said after a deep drag. "A few days later that friendly Shepherd walks by here and sees me in the

177

window. Of course he didn't know I was in the life. I saw his face . . . one large question mark. He stopped in front of the window and then he came in, a dirty grin on his sneaky face. 'How much?' he asked." She snorted again. "Yes that's what he asked *How much?* . . . the dirty . . . the dirty . . ." Words failed her. She took another quick puff from her cigarette and stubbed it out with a nervous gesture.

"I should have thrown him out," she resumed, that's what I *should* have done. I should have told him to go next door. That he . . ." She did not complete the sentence.

"You didn't tell him," concluded DeKok, resignation in his voice. His heart went out to her.

"No, I mentioned an idiotically high figure. That will scare him off, I thought. But he pulled out his wallet and with a poker face he put the money on the table."

She laughed, a bit false, a look of triumph in her eyes.

"It wasn't a success. When it came right down to it, he couldn't do it." She grinned mischievously. "Ordinarily that's no big problem. Lots of men can't do it. They're nervous, scared, put off by the surroundings, or whatever. Some are really impotent, but you find a way to make them comfortable, give them a good time." She shrugged. "It's part of the job."

"Well?" urged DeKok.

"But Mannie was different. First he blamed me, but I would have nothing of that. You should have seen him. Pitiful . . . it's the only word to describe it. There he stood, his pants around his ankles, his face red like a beet. Pitiful." All her contempt was concentrated in that single word. "I looked at him and that's what I said: pitiful and I laughed. He struggled into his clothes and ran from the room. I threw the money after him."

"And you told Alex about it?"

"Yes."

"And Alex?"

She shrugged her shoulders.

"He must have told others. A few days later Shepherd came back and tried to kill me."

"Were you surprised?"

"That he tried to kill me?"

"Yes."

She sank down in a chair and lowered her eyes.

"No," she said softly, "not really. You should never humiliate a man that thoroughly. It's unfair ... it's too easy."

DeKok made his farewells. Just before leaving the room he turned around.

"Make sure to be at the station at ten-thirty tonight."

"Me?" she asked, surprised.

"Yes."

"But why?"

"I want your statement on paper. I also have a few more questions about coffee."

"Coffee?"

DeKok nodded seriously.

"On the day of his death you visited Alex Delzen and made coffee for him. You remember, downstairs in the kitchen."

A wild look came into her eyes.

"So what?"

"Coffee with a lot of sugar," sighed DeKok. "It's not impossible to add poison as well." He paused for effect. "After all," he added deliberately, "you knew it was the last time ... Alex already had another flame."

20

With the shrieking of Ella Rosseling still reverberating in his ears, he put on his raincoat and replaced his hat with slow movements on top of his gray head. Outside the rain had steadily increased and the sky had become darker. Everything was wet, clammy and dreary. The cobblestones along the canal shined in the weak lights of the lamp posts and the trees dripped as hard as the rain, offering no shelter.

DeKok walked along, his hands deep in the pockets of his raincoat, his hat low on his forehead. Where? He had no idea. A thousands thoughts went through his head. He felt himself to be strangely excited and tense. He moved the sleeve of his raincoat a fraction and peered at his watch. The phosphorescent numbers indicated just nine o'clock. He had almost an hour left. Then he would meet with Louise Kamerik and Wim Haverman. Ernst Kluffert and his sister should also be there. Then he would have just half an hour and *she* would be there . . . Ella Rosseling, the little minx.

He walked on. How that girl had screamed at him. Loud, virulent, wild. The reflection of the clear green eyes that seemed filled with a hellish light . . . the light one associated with the glows to be seen around a campfire in the jungle . . . almost supernatural.

Suddenly, in the middle of the quay, he stopped . . . tense, immovable, frozen, like a deer caught in the headlights of a car. He experienced an unseen flash of lighting that stopped him dead in his tracks. A statue in the rain. It took only a moment. Then he seemed to have reached a conclusion. A few seconds later he proceeded, now comfortably settled down in his typical, somewhat waddling gait. A close observer might have detected a faint smile around DeKok's lips.

At the corner he glanced again at his watch. The softly glowing numbers seemed to intrigue him, providing him with a childlike pleasure. He moved on. His eyes sparkled with delight.

* * *

Sergeant Bikerk, the Desk-Sergeant, laughed when he saw a dripping DeKok enter the station.

"That's just incomprehensible," he grinned, "an old professional like you . . . caught in the rain."

DeKok slapped his hat against his thigh, creating a small puddle on the floor. He fished a handkerchief from a pocket and dried his neck.

"Vledder back yet?"

"I haven't seen him."

"Is Dijk on duty?"

"Which one, I've three."

"Robert Antoine."

"Yes, he's on duty. He should be around somewhere. His tour is until two o'clock."

"Excellent, really excellent. When you find him, send him up, please. I'll be upstairs."

DeKok climbed the stairs to the detective room with new-found vitality. He took the stairs two, three steps at a time. There was no sign of painful feet. Upstairs he ignored the few detectives at some of the desks and saw with a certain amount of satisfaction that "his" part of the room was empty. It was at least half a room from his desk to the nearest occupied desk. In his mind's eye he saw it as it would be a little later, when he conducted his "conference". He grinned broadly to himself. It would be a good show.

The door suddenly opened and he saw Robert Antoine Dijk enter the room, briefly glance at some of the desks and then settle his gaze on DeKok. As usual, Robert Antoine was dressed to the nines in a dark-blue suit, black shoes and a pearl-gray tie. He came closer to DeKok's desk.

"Are you going to a party?" asked DeKok.

"My wedding anniversary," nodded Dijk. "My wife and I always celebrate."

"In that suit?"

"It's part of it." Dijk smiled shyly. "My wife is waiting for me. When I get off, we'll have a bite together. Just the two of us . . . some wine, candle light. It's a tradition."

"Since when?"

"Two years. We've been married two years today."

DeKok looked at him and rubbed his eyes. He wondered what the tradition would be like after twenty-five years.

"Well," he said, "I hope it won't get too late, tonight. I wouldn't want to spoil . . . your tradition.

"What do you want me to do?"

DeKok sat down behind his desk and motioned for the young Inspector to sit down as well.

"As you know," he began, "I'm involved in the murder by poison of a young student. Somebody mixed the poison into a tonic the young man was using. This poison, parathion, has not been found during a search of the premises where the murder presumably took place. Of course, it *was* there. In any case, it's of no importance at this time. What I want you to do is the following: You ask the Desk-Sergeant for a uniformed cop and then the two of you take a van to the student house at the Brewers Canal. Park right in front of the house, go inside and announce with a lot of bravura that you're there on orders from Inspector DeKok and you're to pick up all the students in the house for a conference at the station . . . here. I'll give you a list of their names."

He pulled a piece of paper toward him and quickly wrote down the names of the students who resided in the house.

"It's possible," continued DeKok, after he had passed the piece of paper to Dijk, "that Kluffert is no longer there and I'm sure you won't find Haverman there. Don't worry about it, but do make it a point to ask for them. If they tell you they aren't there, you just cross them off the list. But make sure the rest come with you . . . please make sure of that . . . nobody is to be left in the house. Understood."

"No, but I'll do what you want."

"I don't think they'll come willingly," sighed DeKok. "I wouldn't be at all surprised if they had all sorts of objections, excuses, whatever. But you're not to be thwarted. You mustn't listen to them . . . under no circumstances. Act understandingly, but stick to the point. No matter what . . . I want them all here. Without using force, obviously. We can't afford any trouble over this. Your actions are not legal, you must know that. We can't just arrest them. I trust you're inventive enough to come up with some sort of story to make them comply."

"I'll do my best," answered Dijk.

"There's something else." DeKok raised a finger in the air. "And this is important . . . don't forget it! You tell them that I want them here because the premises would have to be evacuated temporarily anyway . . . because of the X-Rays."

"X-Rays?"

"That's what I said . . . X-Rays. Probably the gentlemen will ask what sort of X-Rays."

"Then what."

"You just tell them you don't know."

"But . . . I *don't* know."

"Excellent," smiled DeKok, "really excellent. Then you won't have to lie."

Dijk was now totally confused.

"Bu . . . b-but," he stammered.

DeKok raised a restraining hand.

"But me no buts," he said calmly. "I'll explain later, I promise. But off you go now . . . time is pressing. Make sure you're back here with the whole crowd around half past ten."

"Count on me," said Dijk, stood up and left.

DeKok watched him go and hoped he would be successful.

* * *

Leaning against the front of his desk, DeKok slowly allowed his gaze to travel along the semi-circle of visitors.

They were all there, the members of the Cluster, the macabre murder debates . . . Willem (Wim) Jacob Haverman . . . Johan (Jan) Gelder . . . Emanuel (Mannie) Archibald Shepherd . . . Ernst Kluffert . . . Hendrik (Henk) Jan Marle . . . uncomfortable, apprehensive, restless on straight, steel institutional chairs. Haverman and Shepherd with forced nonchalance, their legs crossed. Gelder leaning slightly forward, attentive, interested. Kluffert and Marle were sitting up straight, pale, visibly tense. Off to one side, lonely and alone, nervously plucking at an invisible thread on her sleeve, was Louise Kamerik, dark-green eyes rimmed in red. Not far from the window, next to a pleased Robert Antoine Dijk, blonde Ria Kluffert was seated, wrapped in an attitude of strong, unapproachable anger, like a *Lorelei* come

185

to life. She stared angrily at Vledder who had forced her to come to the Warmoes Street station. Behind the row of students was Ella Rosseling, provocative, challenging, leaning against a wall. The most colorful personality present.

DeKok's original plan, to encourage a revealing discussion between brother and sister Kluffert had to be scrapped. Ria Kluffert had stubbornly refused to cooperate. She did not, under any circumstances, want to confront her authoritarian brother and had refused to accompany Vledder. Finally, with obvious reluctance, Vledder had been reduced to using force. He had arrested her on the specious charge of "obstructing justice." He knew it would not stick, but it had served the purpose. However, the result had been that the entire crowd had already been gathered by the time Vledder arrived with his "arrestee". There had been no time left for a confidential tete-a-tete.

While DeKok stared at the group he wondered if something could go wrong, if he had made a directing error. In his mind he quickly reviewed all the facts, but could find no gaps. Yet, he was not entirely sure of himself. There were factors which could not be predicted in advance, simply because human emotions could not be classified by laws or formulas. That always remained the uncertainty factor of any investigation. It was ironic that in this case he speculated heavily . . . counted on this emotional uncertainty.

He could not afford to fail. It would be fatal for the case. Everything had to be right, no mistakes were allowed. Vledder saw a grim smile on the otherwise expressionless face of his old mentor. He understood that DeKok had the answers to the puzzle in his mind. The murderer of Alex Delzen was present in the room. But who? Did DeKok know? If so . . . how?

For just a moment Vledder was irritated. As had happened before, he had the terrible empty feeling of being outside the situation, no more than an observer. It was enough to make a grown man cry. Would he ever learn? How long would he still be tied to DeKok's invisible apron strings?

* * *

"Isn't it about time you explain yourself?" Haverman had stood up and gestured with the all-embracing wave of his hands of the future barrister. "I've been here almost an hour. You can't keep us here indefinitely."

"That's right, Mr. Haverman," smiled DeKok. His tone was friendly. "Indeed I cannot. I merely asked you to come here because the house at Brewers Canal, your house, is to be subjected to X- Rays. I call it X-Rays for convenience's sake, because the process is similar to that used for metal detectors at the airport. As I said, since that needs to be done, I thought we might take the opportunity to debate, together, about murder. The subject has, I know, your particular interest."

Haverman sank back in his chair.

"Let's open this gathering," continued DeKok, "by observing two minutes of silence in memory of the two victims. It's because of them that we're here."

He bowed his gray head and remained silent. Meanwhile he wondered if he had taken the right tone, the correct beginning to create the necessary dramatic atmosphere. He looked up after two minutes.

"It is not my habit," he went on, "to create this type of melodramatic ending, among a large of group of people, in order to reveal the solution to a murder case. I'm not an extrovert, no Hercule Poirot. I don't care for this type of scene. But circumstances have left me no other choice. Also, it seemed a good opportunity to lay to rest a number of differences of opinion among you. Perhaps we should call this gathering the 'Epilogue to a Murder'." He paused, rubbed the bridge of his nose with a little finger. "Or perhaps in Latin: *Dura Lex, Sed Lex* . . . The Law is hard, but it's the Law . . . you like that better?"

Haverman looked at him with suspicion.

"The hard Law," he said hesitatingly, ". . . are you trying to say that you're about to arrest the killer?"

"That is correct."

"But, but . . ." Haverman looked dazed. "That means the killer is among us."

"Indeed, Mr. Haverman," sighed DeKok, "Alex Delzen's murderer is in this room." He looked around. "And I know who it is."

Ria Kluffert voiced a scared scream. The sound echoed off the wall and caused some of the other detectives in the room to curiously glance at the group around DeKok's desk. The students looked pale and even Ella Rosseling had a hunted look in her eyes.

DeKok's face was a mask. Even, hard, without expression. From beneath his bushy eyebrows he peered at the group. His glance registered every expression, analyzed every tic, observed every tiny movement.

"Alex Delzen," he continued, louder, "was poisoned by a dose of parathion. Parathion is an agricultural poison, belonging to a group of organic phosphoric-acid esters with anti-cholesteric effects." He looked in Gelder's direction. "Isn't that so, Mr. Gelder?"

"That is correct," said the young biologist.

"Therefore," gestured DeKok, "parathion contains phosphorus and phosphorus . . . you studied gentlemen are erudite enough to know . . . has the capacity to shine, to reflect light. That particular property of phosphorus is generally well know. I would remind you, for instance, of the dial of your watch, an alarm clock and a number of other instruments that glow in the dark.

He remained silent for a moment, out of breath. He had uttered the last few sentences rapidly, without allowing time to think, without breathing.

"And it has been found," said DeKok in a deadly silence, "that parathion, because of the phosphorus it contains, leaves traces, no matter how carefully it has been handled. With the right sort of investigation, these traces will inevitably surface. In short, they light up."

DeKok stopped speaking again, for just a moment. With a dramatic gesture he pointed at the large clock on the wall of the detective room.

"Now," he said, "at this moment, even as we speak, the house at the Brewers Canal is being X-Rayed by a special unit of the Technical Police. I'm not familiar with the exact technique to be used, but as I said, I already know the identity of the killer. The special treatment of the house, will confirm my suspicions and will provide incontrovertible proof, proof which will stand up in a court of law." He looked at each of those present in turn. "We're merely waiting for a phone call. The technical people have been informed of this gathering and have promised to inform me at once. As soon as the call has come through, you may all leave . . . all, except one . . . Alex Delzen's killer."

Tense, DeKok again looked at the group of expectant faces. His fingers drummed nervously against the side of the desk. The sound threatened to burst his eardrums. But when he stopped his fingers with a conscious effort, the silence was so overpowering, so intense, that he hastily resumed his drumming. It was the only sound in the large room. The world seemed to have stopped. Even the usually so noisy Warmoes Street seemed subdued. Slowly the seconds ticked by.

Marle jumped up after a few minutes.

"Why are you torturing us like this?" he exclaimed wildly. "Why? Why don't you just arrest the murderer and let me and the others leave?"

DeKok's eyebrows rippled. Somehow the movement did not seem fascinating at all, but threatening in a way that seemed capable of freezing the blood in one's arteries.

"You, Mr. Marle? Weren't you the man to prescribe a tonic for Delzen?"

"Yes . . . I was."

"Then it will no doubt interest you," snorted DeKok, "that the tonic was used as the vehicle to introduce the poison in Delzen's system."

Marle swallowed a lump in his throat. His eyes were wide and frightened.

"But . . . the tonic," he stammered, "b-but I, I haven't . . . it was . . . I . . ."

DeKok gave him a friendly nod.

"Please relax, Mr. Marle, sit down. You didn't kill Alex Delzen. I know it. You know it. Why should you? You had no reason to kill Alex Delzen. You don't have a sister who . . ."

He was interrupted by Kluffert who jumped up with a contorted face.

"I," he yelled sharply, emotionàlly, "I have a sister." He turned half-way around and stretched an accusing finger in the direction of Ria Kluffert. "There . . . there she is, the little idiot . . . who thinks that at barely eighteen years of age she knows about life . . . about love." His mouth formed an angry grimace. "The dumb . . . the silly creature."

For just a moment it looked as if Ria Kluffert would physically attack her brother. She shook her head vehemently, creating a cloud of spun gold around her head, her eyes flashed and Vledder, next to her, could hear the grinding of her teeth.

DeKok watched calmly. He could not deny that he enjoyed the interplay of opposing emotions "The wrathful Lorelei", he thought, inwardly smiling at the image. Angrily she shook off Vledder's hand, but Robert Antoine Dijk, on her other side, placed a calming hand on her shoulder and that seemed to penetrate. She became more composed.

Ernst Kluffert turned once more toward DeKok.

"I knew," he said, also considerably more under control, "that Alex Delzen had more than a passing interest in my sister. I also knew they met on the sly, although I had strictly forbidden that. I'm no puritan, Mr. DeKok, absolutely not. But I *knew* Alex Delzen and his attitude toward women." He shrugged his shoulders in a helpless gesture. "Ach," he sighed, "I knew that in the end I would lose, could do nothing to stop *her*." He rubbed his forehead and suddenly his eyes flashed with a dangerous light. His expression changed and he assumed the stance of an old-time preacher, preaching everlasting hell and damnation. "But I'm telling you, Mr. DeKok, as God is my witness . . . I would have killed Alex Delzen with my bare hands if he had so much as harmed a hair on my sister's head!"

"And?" asked DeKok simply.

"Eh . . . what?" Kluffert seemed confused, coming out of a daze.

"Did he *harm a hair on her head?*" It sounded laconic.

"No . . . no, not as far as I know."

"So," smiled DeKok, "then you didn't kill Delzen either?"

Kluffert's look seemed devoid of intelligence.

"No," he said dully, shaking his head, "no, not me."

"Excellent," said DeKok, "really excellent. In that case, please sit down again." He rubbed his hands together and looked brightly at the circle of suspects. "The net tightens," he remarked sarcastically. "The number of suspects diminishes." His glance traveled from one to the other. "Is there anybody else who would like to say something? How about you, Mr. Haverman. Didn't Delzen cause you any problems?"

Wim Haverman lowered his head and remained silent.

"Ah, you don't want to talk about it?" DeKok was agreeable. "Very well, perhaps later."

The gray Inspector looked at his watch, demonstratively, and then at the large clock on the wall. He seemed to ponder the discrepancy in times.

"The investigation should just about be completed," he said tiredly. "We can expect the phone call any minute. At most a few more minutes. But this might be the time to correct an oversight. I have forgotten to introduce you to a dear guest." He motioned with a beckoning finger. "Please step forward, Ella."

She detached herself from the wall and approached, hips swaying, breasts bouncing. She passed in front of the row of students, an exciting, beautiful feline.

"This," said DeKok, "is Ella Rosseling . . . an intimate friend of the late Alex Delzen,."

She stood next to him, one hand on her hip, the pelvis slightly thrust forward, her mouth half open and a sultry, sensuous look in her eyes.

"Ella," he asked gently, "do you know any of these gentlemen?"

A faint smile curled around her lips, the males in the room held their breath.

"Yes, I know one of them."

She came closer to DeKok, gripped his arm in a gesture that indicated both availability and the need for protection. All the men in the room felt a stab of jealousy.

"Would you point him out?" asked DeKok.

"Him." She pointed at Shepherd.

"Tell me," urged DeKok, "how you met him."

"Alex introduced him to me."

"Exactly . . . then what?"

She shook her shoulders reluctantly, it did exciting things to her chest.

"Then . . . then nothing."

DeKok smiled down at her.

"Come, come," he said in a cajoling voice. "Didn't he make you a proposition, a few days later?"

"A proposition?"

"Yes, didn't he offer you money for certain . . . eh, favors. I mean, didn't he want to enjoy your feminine charms?"

Ella Rosseling suddenly grinned.

"Oh, yes . . . if that's what you mean . . . yes, he wanted me."

DeKok smiled maliciously.

"And would you like to tell these good people what exactly happened on that occasion?"

Shepherd rose slowly, his face was ashen and his nostrils quivered. His eyes were wide with anger.

"NO!" he roared. "No, you will not . . . you won't!"

He jumped toward Ella, his arms outstretched and his long fingers shaped into claws. There was a gleam of murderous insanity in his eyes.

Ella pressed herself closer to DeKok and screamed.

Suddenly the phone rang, loud, penetrating, overwhelming every other sound in the room. Shepherd froze in place. He became rigid, his mouth half open, his arms still stretched out. DeKok lifted the receiver and listened calmly. A profound tenseness had come over everybody in the room. Kluffert chewed his lower lip, Marle raked his hair.

But all that escaped DeKok. He held his gaze steadily on the cramped figure in front of him. He registered every tiny movement, the slight quiver at the mouth, the labored breathing, the wildly rolling eyes. He watched like a hawk the man he knew capable of murder. Without a word he replaced the receiver after a few seconds.

"Emanuel Shepherd," he said softly, "it's time for a confession."

21

After Emanuel Shepherd had been led away between two uniformed constables, DeKok lowered his head on his crossed arms on top of the desk. He was tired, bone tired, exhausted and empty. The last interrogation had drained him, depleted his reserves. He felt his years. He was no longer thirty when everything seemed to come easy. He raised his head and looked at the young faces of Vledder and Dijk. There was admiration in their eyes and it made him feel good. But it could not banish the lethargy that had overcome him.

"You heard Shepherd's confession," he addressed Vledder. "You can now put it all in a report. Please finish up." With difficulty he raised himself from his chair and waddled over to the coat rack. "I'm going home." He put his hat on and grabbed for his raincoat. "I've had it."

Robert Antoine Dijk hastily took away his coat.

"No," he said, shaking his head. "That's not fair. You're not getting away that easy."

DeKok looked at him.

"Your wife is waiting by candle light."

"She'll just have to wait a few minutes longer," smiled the young Inspector. He studied the old face in front of him. "I'll have them order some coffee from the bar next door, You need it,

I can see that. But before I go, you better answer some questions."

"Am I a suspect?" grinned DeKok half-heartedly.

Robert Antoine picked up the phone and ordered coffee with a shot of cognac. DeKok replaced his hat on the rack and spread his arms wide.

"All right, then," he sighed. "After all, you are entitled to some sort of clarification." He sank down behind his desk. "Help remind me that we go by Duyn in the morning. He should know that Haverman didn't try to stab him ... but that it was Shepherd."

"And that only," said Vledder bitterly, "because Duyn had seen him with a bottle of tonic."

A uniformed colleague arrived with the special coffee from the bar. DeKok looked at him absent-mindedly. He knew most of the force by face, but he could not always find the matching names.

"Brink?" he asked, hesitating.

The constable nodded and placed the tray with three steaming mugs on the desk.

"Weren't you the one who brought in a drunk, about a week ago? The man who later turned out to be poisoned?"

"That was me ... Vries and me."

DeKok gave him a friendly smile.

"Sometimes those things are forgotten among everything else that's going on," he apologized, "but I want to compliment you. That was an excellent report. Very good. Please let Vries know as well. Your report was good enough that it enabled me to catch the killer."

Constable Brink blushed under the weight of that much praise and hastily left the room. Vledder looked at DeKok with astonishment.

"What sort of nonsense is this," he asked, irritated. "You almost never read reports. But I did. I read the report several times and I couldn't see anything exceptional about it."

"What were Alex Delzen's last words?" asked DeKok, reaching out to lift one of the coffee cups.

"His last words . . ."

"Yes."

"Delzen didn't say anything sensible. He was delirious."

"That's not the way it was stated in the report," said DeKok, after his first slurp from the coffee. "There's nothing about being delirious in the report. It's very clearly written. Delzen said *Raskol* . . . and a little later he repeated it again: *Raskol*."

"So . . . what about it?"

"A lot about it. So much in fact, that Delzen used it to try and convey the name of his killer."

"But that's Shepherd!" Vledder was at a loss.

"Exactly," nodded DeKok. "We know that *now*. But you must look at Delzen's last words in the light of what happened before. Delzen didn't realize, until just before he died, that he had been poisoned . . . in other words: murdered. The students had been conducting a number of heated debates about that very subject. Delzen was an important part of those debates. Therefore, it's not unlikely that his last thoughts drifted toward those debates and the many different opinions that had been offered. If Alex Delzen had been less intelligent, he would have named Shepherd. But Alex's brain worked much faster . . . searched for a connection and he came up with Raskolnikoff. Unfortunately he lacked the strength to complete the name."

DeKok looked at his young friend and noticed that Vledder did not get the connection.

"Raskolnikoff," he explained with a sigh, "was the young student in Dostoyevsky's book *Crime and Punishment* who killed an old loan-shark."

"Yes." Vledder's face cleared. "Now I remember something like that. Shepherd defended the murder, didn't he?"

"Not exactly." DeKok shook his head. "He used the murder as an example. You see, *his* example. You should read *Crime and Punishment* sometime, or read it again. For Shepherd there was little difference between himself and Raskolnikoff ... between Delzen and the old loan-shark. Shepherd was heavily in debt to the rich Delzen. You heard his confession. Like Raskolnikoff, Shepherd considered Delzen, the eternal student ... who was intelligent enough but simply didn't care and refused to complete his studies ... he considered Delzen an unnecessary link in society, you see, comparable to the loan-shark in Dostoyevsky's novel. During his last moments Delzen must have realized all that in a flash. That's why, you see, the description he gave of his murderer was so typical, so very apt."

"Raskolnikoff," repeated Vledder, deep in thought. "So, you knew it all along," he concluded.

DeKok rubbed his face, trying to restore some life in it.

"Yes, but only after our conversation with Marle. As of that moment I was almost certain that Shepherd had killed Delzen. I just didn't know how I could force him to confess. Circumstantial evidence, proof, was almost impossible to obtain."

Robert Antoine Dijk was surprised.

"But ... what about the X-Rays?"

DeKok grinned broadly.

"What X-Rays ... nothing ever happened with that."

"No?"

"Of course not. It was just a little trick I played. What do I know about chemical connections, or reactions, or such things. I've no idea whether or not there's phosphorus in parathion, or not. Even less whether it lights up or not. I just needed to get

Shepherd in a certain mood, an atmosphere where he would betray himself. That was the only purpose of the masquerade."

"Goodness." Dijk was completely taken aback. "I really believed you. The way you talked about phosphorus and all that. It sounded convincing." He looked at the older man with respect. "But, what about the phone call?"

"A matter of timing." DeKok shrugged his shoulders, drained the last of his spiked coffee. "I had asked Bikerk to call me at exactly eleven-fifteen. So I watched the time. When it was close to the appointed time, I played my little game with Ella. I knew that Shepherd would get angry . . . it had happened before. The phone call and the outright accusation, completed the job."

Dijk nodded wisely.

"Shepherd lost the will to fight."

Vledder looked intently at his old mentor, studied the tired expression on his face.

"Sometimes," he said slowly, "Sometimes . . . there's something satanic about you."

DeKok stood up, waddled over to the coat rack for the second time. He placed his hat on his head and hoisted himself into his raincoat. Then he turned toward the two young men.

There was a philosophical expression on his face.

"There is a little bit of the Devil," he said softly, "in all of us."

About the Author:

Albert Cornelis Baantjer (BAANTJER) first appeared on the American literary scene in September, 1992 with "DeKok and Murder on the Menu". He was a member of the Amsterdam Municipal Police force for more than 38 years and for more than 25 years he worked Homicide out of the ancient police station at 48 Warmoes Street, on the edge of Amsterdam's Red Light District. The average tenure of an officer in "the busiest police station of Europe" is about five years. Baantjer stayed until his retirement.

His appeal in the United States has been instantaneous and praise for his work has been universal. "If there could be another Maigret-like police detective, he might well be Detective-Inspector DeKok of the Amsterdam police," according to *Bruce Cassiday* of the International Association of Crime Writers. "It's easy to understand the appeal of Amsterdam police detective DeKok," writes *Charles Solomon* of the Los Angeles Times. Baantjer has been described as "a Dutch Conan Doyle" (Publishers Weekly) and has been called "a new major voice in crime fiction in America" (*Ray B. Browne*, CLUES: A Journal of Detection).

Perhaps part of the appeal is because much of Baantjer's fiction is based on real-life (or death) situations encountered during his long police career. He writes with the authority of an expert and with the compassion of a person who has seen too much suffering. He's been there.

The critics and the public have been quick to appreciate the charm and the allure of Baantjer's work. Seven "DeKok's" have been used by the (Dutch) Reader's Digest in their series of condensed books (called "Best Books" in Holland). In his native Holland, with a population of less than 15 million people, Baantjer has sold more than 4 million books and according to the Netherlands Library Information Service, a Baantjer/DeKok is checked out of a library more than 700,000 times per year.

A sampling of American reviews suggests that Baantjer may become as popular in English as he is already in Dutch.

Murder in Amsterdam
Baantjer

The two very first "DeKok" stories for the first time in a single volume, containing *DeKok and the Sunday Strangler* and *DeKok and the Corpse on Christmas Eve*.

First American edition of these European
Best-Sellers in a single volume.

ISBN 1 881164 00 4

From critical reviews of **Murder in Amsterdam**:

If there could be another Maigret-like police detective, he might well be Detective-Inspector DeKok of the Amsterdam police. Similarities to Simenon abound in any critical judgement of Baantjer's work (*Bruce Cassiday*, **International Association of Crime Writers**); The two novellas make an irresistible case for the popularity of the Dutch author. DeKok's maverick personality certainly makes him a compassionate judge of other outsiders and an astute analyst of antisocial behavior (*Marilyn Stasio*, **The New York Times Book Review**); Both stories are very easy to take (**Kirkus Reviews**); Inspector DeKok is part Columbo, part Clouseau, part genius, and part imp. Baantjer has managed to create a figure hapless and honorable, bozoesque and brilliant, but most importantly, a body for whom the reader finds compassion (*Steven Rosen*, **West Coast Review of Books**); Readers of this book will understand why the author is so popular in Holland. His DeKok is a complex, fascinating individual (*Ray Browne*, **CLUES: A Journal of Detection**); This first translation of Baantjer's work into English supports the mystery writer's reputation in his native Holland as a Dutch Conan Doyle. His knowledge of esoterica rivals that of Holmes, but Baantjer wisely uses such trivia infrequently, his main interests clearly being detective work, characterization and moral complexity (**Publishers Weekly**);

DeKok and the Somber Nude
Baantjer

The oldest of the four men turned to DeKok: "You're from Homicide?" DeKok nodded. The man wiped the raindrops from his face, bent down and carefully lifted a corner of the canvas. Slowly the head became visible: a severed girl's head. DeKok felt the blood drain from his face. "Is that all you found?" he asked. "A little further," the man answered sadly, "is the rest." Spread out among the dirt and the refuse were the remaining parts of the body: both arms, the long, slender legs, the petite torso. There was no clothing.

First American edition of this European Best-Seller.

ISBN 1 881164 01 2

From critical reviews of **DeKok and the Somber Nude**:

It's easy to understand the appeal of Amsterdam police detective DeKok; he hides his intelligence behind a phlegmatic demeanor, like an old dog that lazes by the fireplace and only shows his teeth when the house is threatened (*Charles Solomon*, **Los Angeles Times**); A complete success. Like most of Baantjer's stories, this one is convoluted and complex (**CLUES: A Journal of Detection**); Baantjer's laconic, rapid-fire storytelling has spun out a surprisingly complex web of mysteries (**Kirkus Reviews**);

DeKok and the Sorrowing Tomcat
Baantjer

Peter Geffel (Cunning Pete) had to come to a bad end. Even his Mother thought so. Still young, he dies a violent death. Somewhere in the sand dunes that help protect the low lands of the Netherlands he is found by an early jogger, a dagger protruding from his back. The local police cannot find a clue. They inform other jurisdictions via the police telex. In the normal course of events, DeKok (Homicide) receives a copy of the notification. It is the start of a new adventure for DeKok and his inseparable sidekick, Vledder. Baantjer relates the events in his usual, laconic manner and along the way he reveals unexpected insights and fascinating glimpses of the Netherlands.

First American edition of this European Best-Seller.

ISBN 1 881164 05 5

From critical reviews of **DeKok and the Sorrowing Tomcat**:

The pages turn easily and DeKok's offbeat personality keeps readers interested (**Publishers Weekly**). Baantjer is at his very best. There's no better way to spend a hot or a cold day than with this man who radiates pleasure, adventure and overall enjoyment. A ***** rating for this author and this book (**CLUES: A Journal of Detection**).

Also available in hard-cover (bound)

ISBN 1 881164 61 6

DeKok and the Disillusioned Corpse
Baantjer

DeKok watched, flanked by his assistant Vledder, as two men from the coroner's office fished a corpse from the waters of the Brewers Canal. The deceased was a young man with a sympathetic face. Vledder looked and then remarked: "I don't know, but I have the feeling that this one could cause us a lot of trouble. I don't like that strange wound on his head. He also doesn't seem the type to just walk into the water." Vledder was right. Leon, aka Jacques, or Marcel, was the victim of a crime. There are a lot of riddles before the solution is found.

First American edition of this European Best-Seller.

ISBN 1 881164 06 3

From critical reviews of **DeKok and the Disillusioned Corpse**:

Baantjer has provided a fine and profound series of books (*Ray B. Browne*); Baantjer seduces mystery lovers. "Corpse" titillates with its unique and intriguing twists on a familiar theme (*Rapport*, **The West Coast Review of Books**).

DeKok and the Careful Killer
Baantjer

The corpse of a young woman is found in the narrow, barely lit alley in one of the more disreputable areas of Amsterdam. She is dressed in a chinchilla coat; an expensive, leather purse is found near her right shoulder and it looks as if she died of cramps. The body is twisted and distorted. Again DeKok and his invaluable assistant, Vledder, are involved in a new mystery. There are no clues, no motives and, apparently, no perpetrators. But the young woman has been murdered. *That* is certain. Eventually, of course, DeKok unmasks the careful murderer, but not before the reader has taken a trip through the seamier parts of Amsterdam.

First American edition of this European Best-Seller.

ISBN 1 881164 07 1

From critical reviews of **DeKok and the Careful Killer**:

DeKok is ever interesting, a genuine "character". More descriptive, however, is the compassion in DeKok's heart (**CLUES: A Journal of Detection**).

DeKok and the Romantic Murder
Baantjer

At first the murder of Sister Georgette seems a mystery. Who could possibly benefit from killing this nurse, so respected and appreciated by all. Marten is arrested on the night of the murder during an attempted burglary on a bank. His finger prints have been found in the home of Sister Georgette. Naturally he is suspected of the murder. Marten denies the allegation but confesses that he received a letter from the nurse with the request to visit her.

First American edition of this European Best-Seller.

ISBN 1 881164 08 X

From critical reviews of **DeKok and the Romantic Murder**:

A clever false-suspicion story. Everyone should read these stories (**CLUES: A Journal of Detection**). For those of you already familiar with this loveable old curmudgeon, you're sure to enjoy this installment. Score one for the Dutch (*Dorothy Sinclair*, **The Crime Channel**).

DeKok and the Corpse at the Church Wall
Baantjer

Along the wall of the old South Church lies the corpse of a vagrant. At first glance it appears as if the man died of natural causes. But the pathologist discovers different. The man has been murdered in an extraordinary manner. DeKok realizes that he is dealing with an extremely cunning murderer. The dead man is Baron Archibald Manefeldt, rich, eccentric. He enjoys dressing up and living as a clochard, a dock worker . . . but this time!? Was he also a drug dealer? Is that why he was murdered? DeKok encounters a strange family and discovers the trail of the murderer. A second dead Archibald is found! Which is the "real" Baron? Another mystery which forces DeKok to use all his tricks and knowledge.

First American edition of this European Best-Seller.

ISBN 1 881164 10 1

Dective-Inspector DeKok returns in another solid offering from Baantjer (**Publishers Weekly**); DeKok is a careful, compassionate policeman in the tradition of Maigret; crime fans will enjoy this book (**Library Journal**).

DeKok and the Dancing Death
Baantjer

A tall girl, dressed in a multi-colored skirt, an open blouse and long, black hair asks DeKok for a final resting place for her girl friend, Colette. Colette has died of an overdose and has been dead for two days. The body is "stored" in an abandoned building. It is the first in a series of questions that keep DeKok occupied for some time. The questions lead to unexpected answers. It starts with a small, blond boy, found in a cardboard box, next to the dead girl. It leads, via blackmail and addiction, to murder. DeKok's greatest concern is for the child, who he hopes to spare from the fate of his mother.

First American edition of this European Best-Seller.

ISBN 1 881164 11 X

DeKok and Murder on the Menu
Baantjer

On the back of a menu from the Amsterdam Hotel-Restaurant *De Poort van Eden* (Eden's Gate) is found the complete, signed confession of a murder. The perpetrator confesses to the killing of a named blackmailer. Inspector DeKok (Amsterdam Municipal Police, Homicide) and his assistant, Vledder, gain possession of the menu. They remember the unsolved murder of a man whose corpse, with three bullet holes in the chest, was found floating in the waters of the Prince's Canal. A year-old case which was almost immediately turned over to the Narcotics Division. At the time it was considered to be just one more gang-related incident. DeKok and Vledder follow the trail of the menu and soon more victims are found and DeKok and Vledder are in deadly danger themselves. Although the murder was committed in Amsterdam, the case brings them to Rotterdam and other, well-known Dutch cities such as Edam and Maastricht.

First American edition of this European Best-Seller.

ISBN 1 881164 31 4

From critical reviews of **DeKok and Murder on the Menu**:

One of the most successful achievements. DeKok has an excellent sense of humor and grim irony (**CLUES: A Journal of Detection**); Terrific on-duty scenes and dialogue, realistic detective work and the allure of Netherlands locations (**The Book Reader**).